All American Sports Stories

AIRSHIP 27 PRODUCTIONS

All-American Sports Stories Volume One

THE RACER'S EDGE © 2016 Terrence McCauley
FOURTH AND INCHES © 2016 J. Walt Layne
HILLBILLY LIGHTNING © 2016 John Rose
SWITCH © 2016 Fred Adams Jr.
UNCLE BOB'S BROWNING © 2016 Richard Kellogg

Published by Airship 27 Productions
www.airship27.com
www.airship27hangar.com

Interior illustrations © 2016 Art Cooper
Cover illustration © 2016 Shane Evans

Editor: Ron Fortier
Associate Editor: Gordon Dymowski
Marketing and Promotions Manager: Michael Vance
Production and design by Rob Davis.

ISBN-13: 978-0692674192 (Airship 27)
ISBN-10: 0692674195

Printed in the United States of America

10 9 8 7 6 5 4 3 2 1

Contents

THE RACER'S EDGE

By

Terrence McCauley

Indianapolis Motor Speedway
Indianapolis, Indiana 1931

Jericho Welles knew looking at her would only make him feel worse, but he did it anyway.

He had to. Looking at her was part of his penance.

His punishment for being too weak and too poor to be able to stand on his own two feet. For allowing himself and his family to be in a position where he could be corrupted like this.

For allowing such a thing of beauty go to waste. And she was beautiful, at least to a grease monkey like him.

Welles' hands shook as he lifted the hood to take another look at her. He couldn't believe he'd finally been lucky enough to get his hands on something this perfect. And now it was all over before it had even started.

The object of his affection was a big, beautiful, brand new Chrysler Imperial engine. Eight cylinders. Three hundred and eighty-four cubic inches of raw power. Even straight from the factory floor, she would have given him one hundred and thirty-five horsepower at top speed.

But now that Birdy had spent half the night working on her, she would be able to give Welles a whole lot more than that. Birdy was his ride-along mechanic during the race and, next to his wife, the best friend he had in this world.

Birdy had told him the local pit crew they'd just hired had boosted the engine from some big time gambler's car in Cleveland. For an added fee, they agreed to let Welles use her for the race, then put his old engine, an enhanced Ford model, back in when the race was over. That was a good engine, but she couldn't match the power of the brand new Chrysler motor. From that first moment when he'd laid eyes on her, Welles decided he would use his winnings from this race to try to buy her from his pit crew.

Because there had never been any doubt in Jericho Welles' mind that he was going to win this race.

Of course, that had been before Old Man Thompson and his goons had cornered Welles in a quiet area off Gasoline Alley a few hours before. They shoved a bag of money at his chest and told him he was going to have to lose the race. They knew Welles was the odds on favorite to win. But that didn't matter. Carter Thompson, Old Man Thompson's son, was going to shock everyone by being the first across the finish line. If Welles made Carter's victory look convincing enough, there might be more money in it for him after all this was over.

And if he didn't, the goons made it clear he'd never run another race again. One way or the other.

Welles' pride had told him to stuff the money down the old bastard's throat one bill at a time, no matter what the three goons did to him. But he was still holding the bag of cash against his chest when the four men turned and walked away, leaving him with a bag of money and a busted dream.

The shame of that memory brought a knot to Welles' throat. He had been too poor for too long to ever be an arrogant man, but he had never shied away from knowing who and what he was. The good parts and the bad. So it wasn't a matter of pride that made him believe he was one of the best drivers on the circuit.

It was a matter of fact.

Because years of running Archie Doyle's bootleg booze on back country roads on all of those black, moonless nights had honed Welles' driving skills to a fine razor's edge. He had made hundreds of runs from Arkansas to Dallas and Fayetteville and clear up to Detroit and back again. Hell, he could do things with an automobile that most of the drivers on the circuit couldn't do if he taught them.

Welles knew he wasn't just some moonshine hauler. He had a true *racer's* edge.

But once the cops started really clamping down hard on runners, he'd decided to leave the bootlegging life behind. There was a depression on and times were tough all over. In the big cities and in the small towns. Even worse on farms. If he got arrested and went to jail, his family would most likely starve. Sure, Doyle had paid him well enough, but the bigger his family grew, the less attractive danger money became.

That's why he set about put those driving skills to work for himself and his family. He and Birdy had put Arkansas in their rearview mirror and spent the last six months running any race they could find. Between Welles' skills with a wheel and Birdy's skills with engines, they were doing pretty well for themselves. More often than not, they won. And the few times they didn't, they finished in the money. Almost everything they'd earned went back home to their families' farms.

But now, as he looked down at that beautiful gleaming engine, he realized racing had become more to him than just a way to make a buck. Racing had made him understand that he'd never really been a criminal. Speed had always been in his blood, even when he was hauling Doyle's moonshine. And if he was going to risk his neck for his family, he'd rather risk it chasing a dream instead of for some New York fat cat like Doyle.

Welles had entered this race to show the world what he could do. And with an engine like this working for him, he just knew he could win.

But he'd never get the chance, now. Because Old Man Thompson tossed a bag of cash in his lap and his goons backed him up. All that effort – and that beautiful engine – would just go to waste.

And if there was one thing Jericho Welles hated, it was waste.

He reached up and slammed the hood shut. Damned, lousy crooked bastards! It shouldn't have been like this. Racing was supposed to be pure. One man's machine and skill and luck up against the machine and luck of the other men on the track with him. Sure, money could buy better engines and equipment, but once the flag dropped, those advantages disappeared a little with each lap. Tires blew, expensive engines conked out. Drivers panicked or lost control or flat out made mistakes that sent them into the wall.

Sometimes those mistakes cost them their lives.

Welles had spent his whole life doing crooked things for crooked men. And now that life had followed him here. He'd put a lot of effort into changing, but like his daddy used to say: *sometimes the world won't let a man change.*

The dam of tears that had built up behind Welles' eyes broke and he punched the hood. Not in anger, but in frustration. He knew it was just another race, but it was supposed to be *his* race.

It wasn't until the echo of his punch faded in the garage, that he began to hear sounds that had no place in a garage.

Sounds he recognized because he'd heard them before, but not for a long time. Usually before trouble darkened his door.

They were the sound of a man's dress shoes clapping on the garage floor. City man sounds. Rich man sounds.

He wondered if Old Man Thompson and his goons were stopping by to make sure Welles was on board with their plan. Well, he'd be damned if he'd give them the satisfaction of seeing him like this. He pawed at his eyes with the sleeve of his dirty coveralls and turned to face them head on. Yes, he'd take their money, but he'd spit in their eye doing it.

But when he saw who it was, he didn't spit.

He couldn't. His mouth had gone bone dry.

Because Archie Doyle, himself, was standing there smiling up at him. As cocky and dapper as ever.

Welles had always been impressed by the gangster's choice in clothes and that day was no exception. His outfit was perfect for a hot Indianapolis day at the track: a pure white suit and a panama hat cocked at the same rakish angle Doyle wore all his hats. He even had a red flower tucked in the button hole of his lapel. His black dress shoes polished to a high shine. A white outfit was a mighty dangerous thing to wear to a racetrack, but Doyle didn't have a single mark on him. He never did.

If Welles didn't know any better, he would've thought Doyle was just some elegant man of means out for a leisurely day at the races.

But Welles knew better than that. He'd worked for Doyle long enough to know exactly what this man was. And that's why his mouth had gone bone dry.

Because there was no way on earth that this was just a friendly social call.

"Well, well, well," Doyle grinned as he swept off his hat in a grand gesture. "If it ain't the great Jerry Welles himself. How've you been keepin' yourself, Jerry?"

Welles found himself unconsciously wiping his hands on the side of his coveralls. "I'm keepin' myself out of trouble, boss. Best as I can manage."

"Seem to be managin' pretty good, the way I hear it. I understand you're a race car driver now." Doyle used his hat to gesture at the car. "She yours?"

Welles realized he'd put his hand on her, as if to protect her from Doyle somehow. "Yes, boss. Yes, she is."

"Wow. She's a beaut, ain't she? Not that I know much about cars, except how to pay for them. But I always appreciate a man who's an expert in stuff I know nothin' about. Like you with cars, for instance. You always had a way with them. Yes, sir. There's only one man I know who's a better wheel man than you are, but lucky for you, he ain't exactly in the racing game. His interests lie elsewhere."

Welles knew the man who Doyle was talking about. And the thought of that monster being anywhere near him made Welles swallow hard. "Terry Quinn. He…he with you now, boss?"

"Nah. He sat me down one day and told me it was time for him to go off on his own. To pursue his own path, as they say these days. Kinda like you did. Only Quinn did it the right way. He told me he was leavin' and why."

Doyle's grin disappeared. "He didn't sneak out in the middle of the night like some kinda fuckin' rat."

Welles let the rag drop and faced Doyle full on. "I told you I was thinking of leaving, boss. I'd been telling you that for a long, long time."

"Thinkin' and leavin' are two different things in our world, kid. And you lettin' out the way you did without any notice put me in a hell of a bind. That load of 'shine was promised to my people in Cleveland. Took me a couple of days to realize you'd never made that delivery and when I found out, well, I'll admit I was none too happy with you."

Welles figured Doyle had been something way farther north than just unhappy. Then he thought of something that might take the sting out a little. "At least I left all that booze behind."

"Yes, you did." Doyle grinned again. "And that's the only reason why you're still walkin' around today."

Welles didn't doubt it. He also knew full well that Doyle could kill him easily enough right then and there if he had the mind to. Welles was fifteen years younger than Doyle and much taller. But age and size didn't matter much against men like that. Doyle's bootlegging empire stretched from New York all the way to the Midwest.

And men like Doyle didn't let people like Welles slight them.

But Welles didn't want to think about that just then. "How'd you wind up finding me here, boss?"

"I was in town, visitin' an old friend when I happened to hear about this big car race they were havin' this weekend," Doyle told him. "Horse racin's always been more my speed, but my friend told me I'd enjoy this one. I'd never been to a shitkicker soirée before, so I figured I'd give it a whirl, 'specially when I found out how much people bet on these things."

"That's when the gambler in me started askin' questions about who was favored to win the race and why," Doyle went on. "Everyone I talked to kept fallin' all over themselves talkin' about this new kid who was supposed to be a hell of a driver. They told me how he came out of nowhere about six months ago and started tearin' up the tracks in Raleigh and in Durham. Other places, too. That got me real curious, so I asked around, put two and two together and realized that could only add up to one fella: you. You always were a hell of a driver, Jerry. I heard the smart money was on you to leave everyone in the dust here today, too."

Welles thought fast. He couldn't tell Doyle about the fix, but he didn't want the gangster betting a lot of money on him, either. There was no telling what he might do after losing all that money. He decided to not say anything. "That so?"

"I was all set to plunk down a lot of money on you, until a smart guy whispered in my ear and told me to wait. He told me the fix was in and that you'd been paid to let some asshole by the name of Carter Thompson beat you."

Welles closed his eyes and felt a cold sweat break out on his back. "This smart guy got a name?"

"Emmit Thompson. He's the guy I came out here to see."

Welles balled up his fists as he looked away. That son of a bitch wasn't supposed to tell anyone. If Thompson had told Doyle about it, he might have told other people, too. If word got out Welles was crooked, his racing career was through. He wouldn't be allowed into a milk cart derby, much less see another big time again.

"Boss, I know I left you in a lurch by letting out like that, but those federal boys were clamping down hard on runners like me. Had me one too many close calls with the troopers on that last run I did for you to Dallas. I got a mortgage and a family who needs what I earn so…"

Doyle held up his hand. "Relax, kid. Thompson didn't tell anyone. He just thought he was doin' an old friend a favor. Him and me go all the way back to when he was passing that corn whiskey of his for bourbon. Used to peddle the stuff out of the back of those freight trucks he owns. I never drank that rotgut myself, but a good number of folks seemed to like it. I saw a way to make a few bucks from making sure they got it, so I helped him find a market for the stuff in Detroit and other places. Today, the dumb bastard thought he was doin' me a favor by tellin' me about the fix. And he did, too, but not the way he thinks."

Welles didn't know what Doyle meant by that. He wasn't sure he wanted to know. And he was afraid Doyle was about to tell him.

"You're a family man, aren't you, Jerry?" Doyle asked him. "Wife and four kids waitin' for you back home."

Welles felt himself blush. "With another one on the way."

"Jesus," Doyle said. "We've got to get you another hobby. A family that size is a hell of a responsibility. Throw a farm into the mix and you've got yourself a damned expensive proposition."

Welles' back was soaked in sweat and getting wetter. He didn't like Doyle talking this much about his family or his farm. Men like him never engaged in idle chatter. When they said something, it was for a reason and Welles didn't want Doyle talking about his family for any reason. "I…I know I do, boss, and I'll make good on whatever you feel I owe you. I can't give you much from my winnings from this race on account of me not getting any, but…"

Welles stopped breathing when he watched Doyle reach inside that white suit jacket. He started breathing again when all he pulled out was some kind of blue document folded over on itself. He'd seen something like it before, but couldn't place exactly where.

Doyle said, "Your mortgage on that farm of yours is with the First National Bank of Hot Springs, ain't it, Jerry?"

Welles didn't like where this was going. "Yes, boss, it is. I…"

"Well, today must be your lucky day, kid, because you just happen to be talkin' to the man who bought the First National Bank of Hot Springs about two months ago. I'm settin' up shop in Hot Springs this fall and I figured a bank would be a nice bit of business for a fella like me to own." He waived the blue document. "And it also just so happens that I've got your mortgage right here in my hand."

He handed it to Welles who took it and read it. The man wasn't lying. It was his mortgage all right.

"Boss, I swear, I'll…"

Doyle snatched the mortgage back from him. "Shut up. You've said your peace now I'll say mine. Emmitt Thompson and I have done business for years, but he's recently gotten too big for his own good. He's gone and opened up a side channel for his booze with Capone's old outfit up in Chicago. The dumb bastard figured I'd never find out about it. But he forgot that I find out about everything eventually."

"And, in case you haven't figured it out already, I hate sneaks who do things behind my back. Emmit told me he's got a lot riding on his son winning this race today on account of the fix being in. He's bet more than he can afford to lose. I know for a fact that he plans on using his winnings from today's race to set up more stills and buy more trucks so he can move more hooch to his new friends in Chicago.

"But I don't want him doin' that," Doyle went on. "I make good coin on his current operation, so I want him to keep on bein' dependent on me for distribution. So you understand what I need you to do for me?"

Welles thought he did, but he wanted Doyle to spell it out.

And Doyle obliged. "You say you're willin' to pay me back for walkin' out on me so sudden. Then prove it by goin' out there and winnin' this race like you're supposed to. Because if you don't," he waived the mortgage again, "you can say good bye to that dirt patch you call a farm because you and your family'll have to find another place to live. And in case you ain't been readin' the papers lately, these ain't exactly the best times to be homeless."

Welles choked down the anger rising inside him. "And if I win?"

"When you win," Doyle corrected him, "I'll tear up your mortgage and all debts are forgiven. Hell, I'll even give you a cut of my winnings after I bet on you today. You know how generous I can be when I'm in a good mood. And puttin' a sneak like Emmitt Thompson in his place will put me in one hell of a fine mood."

Welles didn't see as how he had much of a choice. As rotten as he knew Thompson could be, Doyle was much, much worse. "It won't put Mr. Thompson in a very good mood, though. He'll be pretty sore at me after all this is over."

"I wouldn't worry much about him, kid." Doyle put the mortgage document back in his pocket. "I'd worry about me."

●●●

Welles' hands were still shaking when Birdy and the new pit crew boss came into the garage. The boss was a local guy Birdie knew who called himself Butch. Looked like a Butch should, too. Big, nasty looking bastard with a permanent stubble sprinkled with gray and hard, deep set eyes.

Birdie had known Welles long enough to know something was wrong the moment he laid eyes on him. "What happened, champ?"

Welles looked at Butch and said, "Could you give me a minute alone with Birdy? There's some stuff I have to tell him that don't concern you."

Butch folded his arms and leaned against the racecar. "I'm not going anywhere, friend. If it's got something to do with this race, then it's got something to do with me."

"Butch is a good egg, Jerry," Birdy told him. "We did time in Joliet together. You can speak freely around him."

Welles didn't like it, but he didn't see as he had much of a choice. He knew the fear and worry about the spot he was in would only keep eating at him unless he told someone about it. And Birdie was the best person he could think of to listen.

Welles told them everything. About Thompson and about Doyle. Neither man said anything until he'd finished laying it all out for them.

When he was finished, Birdy pushed his cap back on his head. "Sounds like a hell of a morning." He leaned against the car next to Butch. "What do you want to do about it, champ?"

Butch made a suggestion. "We can split the difference and pull you out of the race if you want. It's not the way I'd like to see you go out, but it might be the safest."

"No chance," Welles said. "Doyle would see that coming a mile away. Even if it were true, he'd never believe it. Besides, Thompson might be king shit in these parts, but Doyle's got an operation that stretches from here to New York City. Running out on him now would only make him madder at me than he already is. And I can't risk him foreclosing on my farm if I run out on him." He thought about it again and made up his mind. "No, I've got to not only run the race, but I've got to win it, too. There's just no other way out of it."

Butch grinned and slapped him hard on the back. "That's the spirit, Jerry. Never say die. I like you already."

Birdy said: "Sounds like you've got a race to win, doesn't it, champ?"

"Yeah." And for the first time that day, Jericho Welles smiled. "Yeah, it sure does, doesn't it?"

●●●

After Butch went to his crew in the pit, Birdy and Welles got ready for the race the same way they'd gotten ready for all their races before. Some of the other drivers had fancy head gear and goggles and nice white scarves to throw around their necks for an added dash as they sped around the track.

Birdy and Welles had a couple of old leather football helmets they'd used back in high school. Neither of them had ever gotten around to graduating, but they'd been there long enough to play on the football team. They had a pair of goggles they'd gotten from an old crop duster they'd known from the next county over. The old coot told them he'd worn those goggles when he shot down German planes in France, but neither Birdy or Welles believed it.

Most of the other drivers wore pure white coveralls. But, despite Welles' objections and the heat of the late May day, Birdy and Welles put on old leather jackets. Birdy was convinced the leather would help them survive if they crashed and got thrown from the car. Not that Welles had any intention of crashing, mind you. But he hadn't intended on a lot of things that had happened to him that day.

Yes, Welles thought. Racing sure was a damned unpredictable sport if there ever was one.

Birdy looked under the hood while Welles hopped in behind the wheel. He hit the ignition and gave it one final rev before they pushed the car out onto the track. Welles felt comforted, almost happy as he felt all six

"Sounds like you've got a race to win, doesn't it, champ?"

cylinders firing like they were supposed to. The entire car shook, like a long sleeping thing coming alive once more.

Most of the other drivers he'd met on the circuit only cared about the size of their engines, figuring speed and power were enough to carry them through the five hundred laps to victory.

But Jericho Welles knew it took much more than that. Even back when he was just a rum runner, he'd seen how big engines could take a curve too quick; sending both car and driver sailing off the road into a ditch or worse: off into a holler. He'd learned long ago that good brakes and tight handling are every bit as important as speed. Maybe even more important. That's why he and Birdy always made sure that any car he raced had breaks that were in top notch condition and that the wheel was tight enough to turn the car on a dime.

Birdy closed the hood and gave him the thumbs up. He yelled over the roar of the engine: "She sounds good to me, champ."

Welles killed the ignition. "Yeah. She sure does, doesn't she?"

●●●

With Welles on one side and Birdy on the other, they pushed the car toward the Number Eight spot on the track. Welles used his free hand to steer the wheel and keep the car on course. Other teams were doing the same thing, racking up racecars like balls on a billiard table. They'd all hold their places, too, on that first lap around the track, right up until the pace car eased off to the pit side. That's when the race really began.

Welles knew he should be excited or even anxious at times like these. Every race was different and no one could ever fully predict what might happen. But Welles never felt much of anything as he and Birdy pushed their car into contention. If anything, he felt resigned. Damned near peaceful in fact. He had reason to be. He knew that, in Birdy, he had the best mechanic on the course. And he knew he was one of the best drivers out there. He was used to hauling a sedan full of booze at top speeds around the hairpin turns of back country roads from Arkansas to Baton Rouge and from Fort Worth all the way up to Colorado. Almost all of his runs had been made at night when the cops were sleepy and there were fewer cars on the road. Sometimes he'd made whole runs without the benefit of headlights.

A good number of the other drivers on the circuit had been rumrunners, too. The difference was they weren't Jericho Welles. He'd moved more moonshine and bootleg liquor faster and farther than anyone else on Doyle's payroll. He'd been shot at, chased, threatened and scared out of his mind.

But he'd never been caught and he'd never missed a deadline. Except for the last delivery he was supposed to make for Doyle.

And as he pushed the car into position, he realized he'd never gone back on his word. Ever. He knew he'd made an arrangement with Thompson to throw the race. He'd taken the man's money and there was a part of him that didn't like going back on a deal. Even a crooked deal he'd made virtually at gun point with Old Man Thompson.

But there was a part of Welles, a bigger part of him, that hated losing even more. Butch had been right. He was in this race and he was in it to win.

Welles needed to talk about something, anything else that would distract himself from thinking about Doyle and Thompson. He asked Birdy: "You sure Butch got the pit crew squared away?"

Birdy nodded quickly as he gasped for breath. The car wasn't that hard to push, but Birdy had never been the durable kind. "Butch swears up and down that they're the best pit crew booze can buy. They're all ex-car thieves like Butch, so they shouldn't have much trouble getting us out of the pit in good time. Says they're better than average when they're sober and he won't let them touch a drop until the race is over."

Welles didn't like banking his chances of winning on a crew of drunken convicts. But he wasn't in a position to be choosey. "Then let's hope they stay sober."

"Hell, Jerry. I'm more worried about you than I am about them," Birdy said. "You've got yourself in a hell of a situation here, son. You sure you're gonna be ok to run this thing? I don't care what Butch thinks. If you want to run, I'll run with you."

Welles knew he should've been touched by the offer, but his mind was too busy for sentiment to reach it. "Just keep pushing, Birdy. Keep pushing."

●●●

When they got the car to the eighth spot, Welles could see Carter Thompson had already pushed his car into the pole position. He'd won the spot fair and square by having the best time in yesterday's qualifying round. Carter usually had the pole position in all of his races, preferring to lead from the front and stay there.

But what Carter saw as his greatest strength, Welles saw as his greatest weakness. The boy was a good driver, but he needed to be first. Always and at all costs. He'd won a lot of races in his time, but never against Welles.

He figured Old Man Thompson must've told his boy about the fix. He also figured Carter would be feeling mighty good about his chances right about then. That's why Welles did his best to avoid making eye contact with the boy. There was still about a half an hour until the race started. He didn't want Carter sensing anything might be wrong with the arrangement he made with his father.

Welles was a lot of things, most of them not very good, but he'd never been able to lie worth a damn. And he knew one slip up in front of Carter would complicate things in a big way.

And things were plenty damned complicated enough already.

• • •

Welles was helping Birdy make some last minute adjustments to the steering when he felt Carter saunter over behind them. "Great day for racing, ain't it, boys?"

"Sure is," Welles said as he stood up. He felt the heat rising from the asphalt in waves, baking men and machine alike. Thanks to the leather jackets, Welles could feel a thin layer of sweat all over his body.

But Carter looked fresh as a daisy. He radiated wealth and money, but not the kind of wealth and money men like Emmet Thompson or Archie Doyle had. Both of them might've been bastards, but at least they'd earned every crooked penny they had. Welles could see that Carter had the oblivious indifference of inherited wealth. Pink cheeks, dirty blonde hair and clear blue eyes. He was one of those young men who raced for sport, not profit.

Racing was a hobby to him. And to Welles, racing was a way to make a living.

No, Welles decided. They couldn't be more different if one of them had been from Earth and the other from Mars.

"I'll admit you got me baffled, though." Carter motioned to Welles' leather jacket. "I never could understand why you boys always go with leather. Rain or shine, cold or hot, you two never race without it. Why is that?"

Welles explained it. "Birdy says leather's better at keeping us from getting cut up by the asphalt in case we get thrown."

Carter laughed, but it wasn't the kind of laugh Welles knew or liked. It was a cultured laugh. A polite laugh. No, Welles didn't like it one bit.

Carter said: "Seeing the milk crate you're running in today, looks to me like you'll need all the leather you can get."

Birdy popped up from under the steering wheel and said, "I'll give you some leather, you arrogant son of a...." But Welles gently eased him back down to return to his work.

If Carter noticed Birdy's outburst, he didn't let on. "What've you have under there, anyway? I hear it's a supped up Ford engine."

Welles saw no reason to correct him, but saw every reason to build up his ego a bit. "You hear pretty good, Carter." He could tell Carter was dying to tell him about his car, so he gave in and asked, "What about you?"

"A D.O. Dudda engine custom with a double overhead-cam built by Gus Dudda himself." Carter actually rocked up on his toes as he said, "Gus happens to be a good friend of the family."

Welles was impressed but didn't show it. Dudda was a damned fine engine if you knew how to handle the power just right. And he wondered if Carter knew how. "Sounds like you've got yourself a hell of an automobile. Best of luck out there today."

Carter laughed that grating laugh again. "Luck's for suckers, Jerry. You know that. Why take chances when you can have a sure thing in your back pocket?" He lowered his voice as he held out his hand to Welles. "No hard feelings about the way things will turn out today, I hope."

Welles smiled as he shook the boy's hand. He saw a way of getting into the boys head a little, so he said, "That's the funny thing about the racing business, Carter. There's just no telling what'll happen out there once the flag drops. You'd do well to remember that."

When Carter went back to his car, Birdy said: "That little son of a bitch needs a good dressing down, don't he? Still, you didn't do us no favors by saying that to him. One word to his daddy and we're in a bad way."

But Welles was in no mood to debate. "Keep working, Bird Man. Keep working."

●●●

Welles climbed in behind the wheel and fired up the engine. Birdy got in the passenger seat to his left and hunkered down as low as he could get. As the ride along mechanic, he'd be Welles' eyes and ears on the race course, reading gauges, judging the other racers. Seeing what Welles might not be able to see on the race course. He'd also make whatever repairs he could to the car while they were out on the course between pit stops.

Unlike Carter, Welles had held back on showing everyone what the engine could do on the qualifying lap the day before. He'd held back on purpose, but he knew what the engine could do. He didn't need to rev her. He just fed her enough gas to warm her up so she wouldn't be cold before the flag dropped.

He'd learned that races were won on handling and fuel consumption. No reason to waste gas on revving the engine for the pleasure of the crowd.

Yet, as was his custom, Welles looked at the crowd in the closing minutes before race time. The grandstand was packed with spectators who looked like they'd come from miles around to spend the afternoon watching these forty cars race five hundred miles on a single track. Five hundred laps of speed and fury where anything could happen at any given moment and quite often did. Ask any of the men, women and children why they were there that day, they would tell you they were there to see the race. Maybe enjoy a hot dog and a Coca-Cola and some popping corn in the process.

But Welles knew better. He knew what they'd really come to see was the carnage. Engines seized, tires blew. Cars bumped into each other and smashed into the wall. Sure, they cheered long and loud for the winner at the end, but from the moment the flag dropped until they waived the checkered flag, every single one of them rooted for disaster. And the death that often came with it.

Welles and all the other drivers knew the crowd probably wouldn't be disappointed. But Welles, like every other driver, just hoped and prayed he wouldn't be the one who gave the bastards what they wanted.

●●●

Birdy had to shout so Welles could hear him over the increasing roar of the engines from the other cars. "Keep an eye on the ninth and tenth positions behind us. I watched them on the qualifying run yesterday. It looked to me like both cars tend to pull to over to the left. If they get boxed in, they might overcompensate and bump you while they're doing it."

Welles slipped his goggles over his eyes. "What do you think about Carter?"

"That Dudda he mentioned is custom-built for speed. So don't be surprised if he rushes to take the lead at first. If he does, he's good enough to hold it for a good long while. But I've got a feeling the kid gets real cocky real fast, so you can probably take him later in the race. But he's liable to panic when you come on strong, so you'll have to give him room when you make your move."

Welles gripped the wheel tighter. "I don't have to give him a goddamned thing."

Birdy smiled as he slid his own goggles into place. "No, I suppose you don't."

●●●

The flag finally dropped and the pace car slowly took the cars out for the ceremonial first lap around the track. All the cars held their positions at first, struggling against the slower pace like racehorses straining against the bit.

Welles watched Carter in the pole position nose the pace car just a little. He didn't get close enough to be fined for it, but closer than he was supposed to be.

The roar of the crowd grew louder and louder as the pace car gently eased off the track and every driver on the course shifted into higher gear as they hit the gas. Forty highly-tuned automobiles, built for maximum speed and distance, controlled by their drivers, surged together at once as if they were all a part of some living, speeding thing.

Because for that brief moment in time, they were.

The race was under way.

As the first few laps rolled by, Welles was pleased that his vehicle was handling just the way he and Birdy had planned. She moved faster and smoother around the turns of the racetrack than any other car he'd driven. She didn't buffet and she didn't shimmy. She switched gears like a dream and gave him all the speed he asked for. Her wheel was responsive as hell as he edged her from left turn to left turn around the course.

All thoughts of Doyle and Thompson slipped from his mind. This was something men like that could never understand. This was racing. And these were the moments Jericho Welles lived for.

Those early laps of the race were no different than any of the other races Welles had run. The drivers of many of the cars held back, choosing to hold something in reserve for the latter part of the race. Other cars drifted toward the back of the pack because, for some reason or another, they had problems holding course.

Welles put their misfortune to work for him as he was able to gradually move up four places and take sole possession of the fourth position. Carter Thompson had held the lead since the beginning and showed no signs of letting up.

But that didn't bother Welles. In fact, he'd never worried much about where he was in the course of a race, so long as he was the first one across the finish line when they waived that checkered flag.

Although he was too busy driving the car to know the number of laps he had left, keeping track was Birdy's job, he could tell he was well within the first third of the race. That's when he heard Birdy call out: "Looks like one of the cars in the back just blew an engine."

His years of bootleg driving on dark country roads had taught Welles how to make the most of the brief glances he made in rear and side view mirrors.

And one glance in the rearview mirror told Welles all he needed to know.

He saw a thick column of steam billowing out from under the hood of a car on the high ride side of the track way at the back of the pack. The steam was thick enough to blind the driver and most likely, scalding the poor bastard in the process. Welles saw him throw up his hands to protect his face and watched the car veer wild to the left, taking out the last two cars in the race with him. One car slammed into the front of the steaming car and jack-knifed up into the air: tumbling end over end until it slammed down on all four wheels on the grassy area in the middle of the raceway. The two other cars spun out onto the grass as well, some forty yards away from the wreck.

If this had been a normal Sunday afternoon drive with his family, Welles would've pulled over and helped the men from the wreck. He would have had compassion for the brave men and their broken machines that were now out of the race.

But competition had always gotten the better part of compassion in Jericho Welles. And this wasn't a quiet Sunday drive with his family. This was a race. A race he was going to win.

For his family. For himself.

He boiled down the consequences of what had just happened into cold mathematics. Three cars down meant there were thirty-seven cars still on the track. Thirty-six other drivers and ride-along mechanics and their machines standing in his way to victory.

As the number of laps kept piling up, Welles could feel the car was getting more and more difficult to control. Birdy did what he could to tighten the handling, but both men knew it was more than that.

The heat rising from the asphalt and the heat from the constant speed of the race were beginning to take their toll on the tires. The tight handling and the balance he needed was disappearing rapidly and he found himself battling with another car to maintain fourth place. There was only one way to solve the problem: they'd have to change out the tires and soon or risk a blow out. At speeds of thirty miles an hour, a blow out could be problematic. At speeds of well over one hundred and twenty miles an hour, a blow out was quite often deadly.

Deciding when to pit was Birdy's job. He knew the car better than anyone. Until then, Welles concentrated on driving, making sure he stayed as close to the head of the pack as he could while maintaining a good distance between himself and the other cars around him. At speeds like this, even the slightest bump could prove to be disastrous.

Lap after lap, Welles tried keeping his mind fresh. He knew driver fatigue was every bit as dangerous as mechanical fatigue. Maybe even more so. It was easy for men to let their brains lock up, to almost become hypnotized by the circular, monotonous pace of a circular race around the same track. Speed was as seductive as it was deadly. It could easily lull even the best drivers into a trance.

That's why Welles kept himself fresh. He was careful to keep moving his eyes every few seconds. He kept checking his mirrors. He turned his head every once in a while to keep track of where the cars were running around him.

Every glance told him how the race was evolving. And as the number of laps added up, he saw more and more cars fall by the wayside. One blew his right tire going into a turn, careening off the wall before sliding left until it trailed all the way off the track. Several more simply just pulled into the pit area and never re-entered the race.

Despite even his best efforts, Welles felt his mind beginning to drift, so he called out to Birdy over the roar of his engine. "What's the disposition?"

"We're whittling them down, champ," he called back. "We're down to twenty-seven cars all told. Thompson's still in the lead and running well. The heat coming off the track is playing hell with everyone's tires."

"What about us?" Welles yelled. "How are we doing?"

"Gauges all still look good. Fuel's a bit low, but she's burning better than I thought she would. I'm more worried about the tires. I'd give us five more laps before we have to head into the pit."

He kept checking his mirrors to track the cars running around him.

Welles shook him off. The wheel felt a bit sluggish in his hands but not much. "These babies still have about seven good laps left in them at least."

Birdy muttered curses under his breath as he reached for the wireless to contact the pit crew. He held the earpiece up to his ear as he yelled into the microphone. "Butch? Come in Butch." Butch's garbled response came over the air, so Birdy yelled, "We'll be coming in for a tire change and to refuel in about seven laps or so. Get your crew ready." A pause while Butch responded, then, "I know, I know. I told him that. But he's one stubborn son of a bitch."

Welles smiled as he hit the gas coming out of a turn.

●●●

As soon as Welles brought the car to a screeching halt in the pit area, he was surprised how ready the pit crew was. Birdy popped out of the car to direct the two men who began to replace the rear tires on the car while another man began to refuel her.

Butch threw a big jar of ice cold water in Welles' face, then handed him another to drink. "Drink that down," he barked. "It'll clear your head, keep you focused."

Birdy opened the hood and Butch leaned in with him. "She's running hot as hell but she's still handling like a dream."

"Of course she is," Butch said. "I worked on this baby myself. My cars always handle like a dream. That engine's the least of your worries."

Welles didn't like that. "And just what the hell is that supposed to mean?"

"I heard that the Thompson team thinks something's up with you. Said they don't like how you're hanging around the front of the pack so much for so long. I heard they'd feel a whole lot better if you'd lay off and quit crowding Carter so much."

"That's too damned bad," Welles said, "because I'm gonna crowd him a whole lot more."

The fuel man screwed the cap back on as the tire men started to replace the front two tires. Birdy slammed the hood shut and scrambled back into the passenger seat. "You won't be crowding nobody if we don't get back out there!" To the tire men he said, "Let's go boys! Faster with them tires!"

The tire men had just taken the car off the jack and were tightening up the lug nuts as Butch told him, "She's running hotter than I'd like, so let up on her in the turns to conserve water. And I'll keep you posted on the wireless if I hear anything more on Thompson. The bastards might be listening in, so I'll say 'red flag' if I hear something I can't tell you."

The tire men cleared the car as if it was on fire. Butch slapped the end of the car like she was a racehorse. "Now go, goddamn it. Go, go, go!"

The gauges on the dashboard jumped to life as Welles hit the gas slow and steady. A lot of drivers pealed out of pit row as fast as they good, leaving skid marks on the asphalt. It looked great for the crowd, but Welles knew it left valuable rubber in the pit instead of on the tires where it belonged.

He built up speed slowly but steadily until he cleared the pit and hit the track. It would take a good lap or two before the car was back up to speed, but it saved wear and tear on the engine.

With a full tank of gas and four new tires, the car felt better than before. She felt broken in and hungry for speed. After a few more laps, Birdy told him: "We're now in fifth place and coming up strong on fourth. Damned nice work, champ."

Welles smiled. "Not bad for a stubborn son of a bitch, is it?"

Birdy high pitched cackle rose over the roar of the engine. "No, not too bad at all."

Welles slid in behind the number four car, hearing the roar of the crowd as he sped past the grandstand. Their smiling faces and waiving arms little more than a blur he saw out of the corner of his eye. He knew the bastards loved a challenge for position.

He nosed the car up close to the number four car, but not close enough to touch it. In the turn, he eased the car to the right, the high end of the track, and let the fourth car's drag sling shot him ahead of him. Doing this made the lead car consume more gas while helping Welles save some.

"Back where we started!" Birdy cheered as they shot into forth place on the straightaway. Now feed her some gas and let's tail that number three car for a spell. And give Old Man Thompson the fidgets!"

Welles knew strategy was Birdy's job, but he wasn't the man behind the wheel. The lead three cars were grouped in a tight back, a good four seconds ahead of him. None of them had made a pit stop yet. He knew each of them was well overdue for fuel and new tires. Especially Carter since he'd been in the lead since the start.

Welles called out to Birdy: "Any of them make a pit stop yet?"

"Not that I've seen."

"Why do you think that is?"

"Can't rightly say," Birdy yelled. "This heat should've sent them in for a tire change by now. Maybe…"

Welles was about to go into a turn when he saw the number two car, already in the turn ahead of him, blow out both front and rear tires on the right side. He figured the extra weight of the car on that side in the turn and the heat of the worn tires must've done it.

The third car zoomed around him and into second as the wounded car collapsed on its right side like a wounded horse, sending sparks shooting out behind it as the metal of the wheels grinded against the asphalt. Gravity, speed and momentum all worked against the driver, combining to flip the car sideways and send it tumbling in the air, landing first, upside down, then back on its left side against the wall.

Right in front of Welles' speeding car.

Instinct and adrenaline kicked in all at the same time. In one fluid motion, Welles checked his mirrors and, seeing other cars bearing down on his left, he had no choice but to do the unthinkable. He jerked the wheel to his right as he hit the gas. He shot through the narrow gap between the wreck and the wall, with inches, maybe even centimeters to spare.

He cleared the wreck and avoided the wall, slinging back down to the left side of the track as he came into the straightaway out of the turn.

Now Welles found himself all alone in third place. And was gaining on the lead two cars.

The crowd cheered as much for his maneuver as they did for the wreck just as the yellow caution flag went up. The pace car bolted out onto the track to control the pace of the race. All the drivers now had to stay locked in their positions at a reduced speed until the wreck was cleared by the racing and track crews.

Welles knew the people in the stands had the luxury of speculating whether or not the wrecked car was done for the day. And if the driver and his ride along mechanic were still alive. But Welles and Birdy and the other drivers on the course didn't have that luxury. Neither of them mentioned the wreck. Neither of them even thought about it. Neither of them dared. To do so would've acknowledged the worse that could happen in a race like this. And men didn't win races by focusing on the worst.

They won by focusing on the race. By focusing on what it took to win. By being the best.

Besides, Welles and Birdy were now running in third place.

About a dozen or more laps passed under the caution flag as the crews worked fast to pull the wreck off the track. Other crews cleared the raceway of shredded tires and debris as best they could for the safety of the remaining drivers. They took their time and no one complained. Because at speeds of over a hundred miles an hour, even a small shard of metal or a forgotten bolt could prove lethal to both man and machine.

Welles and Birdy saw the dark brown stains on the track as they passed the site of the crash once the car was pulled away.

Neither of them would admit it.

After the wreckage and all of its remnants were cleared, the pace car drifted off the track toward the pit area and all the cars began to pick up speed. The crowd roared again. The race was back on.

And then Welles saw Carter Thompson's car trail off the track behind the pace car to take his pit change.

"He might be a no good spoiled brat," Birdy observed, "but he's a smart bastard. While it'll take everyone a couple of laps for everyone to get back up to speed, he'll pop out of the pit fresh as a daisy and won't miss much. Smart, smart boy."

But Carter would miss much, Welles thought. He'd lose the lead. And Welles would be damned if he'd give it back easily.

Because now he was in second place.

●●●

It stayed like that for a good long while and Welles didn't complain. Lap after lap, he was happy to trail the lead car in a comfortable second place. There was plenty of time left. More than a third of the race. Plenty of time for Carter Thompson to make his move.

The rest of the pack had fallen off a bit by then, biding their time while they hoped for a blow out or a seized engine among the two lead cars at the head of the pack. There were 500 laps in this race for a reason. Every single second of every single one of them counted.

Welles knew all about the man driving the lead car in front of him. He was a man by the name of Bill Milano and he was a damned good driver. Cool customer, too. Word was he'd been the best wheel man in the Cleveland mob once upon a time, and he, like Welles, was smart enough to get out of the game before the law caught up with him. Where Carter Thompson had learned racing on the track as a hobby, men like Welles and Milano had learned to drive fast as a way of life.

Welles knew Bill and liked him. A lot. But he wouldn't let his friendship or his admiration cause him to lose to him. Or to anyone else for that matter.

Because he was a race-car driver now. This was who and what he was now. Racing was all he had and all he wanted. He wouldn't throw it away for anyone. He only hoped Archie Doyle would keep Old Man Thompson off him long enough to get out of Indianapolis when all of this was over.

Welles' knew his mind was starting to drift again and he snapped himself out of it by asking Birdy, "What's Carter up to?"

Birdy checked the mirrors first, then turned to look behind them. "He's in the rocking chair back between the fourth and sixth guy. He's taking plenty of drag and letting it pull him around the track. Bastard's probably saving up to make a run for it when we pit."

Welles hated to admit it, but he was impressed. "You know, beating him would be a hell of a lot easier if he wasn't so good at this."

"You'll beat him, though," Birdy said. "And that's what worries me."

But Welles didn't have time to think about that now. "When do you want to pit?"

"That caution flag saved wear and tear on our tires and our fuel. Still, I'd like to pit in another ten laps or so, refuel and slap on new treads so we can have plenty to give Carter and Milano a run for their money come the finish."

But Welles surprised Birdy by managing to hold his second place spot and get another twenty laps out of the tires and his fuel before he decided to head into the pit. He wanted to be as fresh as possible for that last leg of the race.

And just as he eased into the pit lane, Welles watched Carter Thompson shoot around the cars in front of him as he took second and made a strong play for Milano and the lead.

Welles screeched to a halt as Butch and the pit crew descended on the car again with water and fuel and new tires.

Butch threw another jar of water in Welles' face and handed him another jar.

Welles pawed at his wet face with the back of his hand. "I sure wish you'd quit doing that."

"Keeps you alert," Butch said as he and Birdy went to work on the engine. "And you're gonna need all the help you can get. I heard Old Man Thompson's awfully nervous you're not going to throw this thing, so he's put out something of a bounty on you boys."

Welles stopped drinking his water. "A bounty? What kind of bounty?"

"I didn't manage to get an exact dollar amount," Butch told him, "but he's put the word out that any driver who keeps you from winning the race gets a bonus. Knock you out, wreck you, box you in. It doesn't matter, just so long as you don't beat Carter."

"He can't do that!" Birdy yelled from under the hood. The racing association will…"

"He is the racing association," Butch said. "Why do you think Carter doesn't have to pit so much? Because he's got a bigger tank and thicker wheels than everyone else is why. The little bastard's got an unfair advantage on the rest of us."

Welles knew something had been up. "Haven't the other drivers or pit crews complained?"

"Sure they have," Butch said, "but who's gonna listen? There ain't much anyone can do about it. Not when his old man is the commissioner."

Welles knew he should've been angry or scared. Something! But the truth was that he didn't feel anything at that moment. Sure a bigger tank and thicker tires gave Carter a hell of an edge, but an edge wasn't a guarantee. Carter was a good driver, but advantages be damned: Welles knew he was better.

And he didn't suffer from the one glaring weakness Carter did.

Pride.

And Welles knew pride was how he was going to beat him.

Butch and Birdy slammed the hood shut as the boys tightened up the nuts on the front wheels of the car. Welles said, "Butch, we're going to need your eyes down here to see what we can't. You see someone pulling anything, you tell us over the wireless. No code words, no secrets. Just shout it out there. I don't care who hears."

"I will." The final nut on the tire was tightened as the fuel man pulled away. Butch slapped the ass of the car one final time. "Now go, go, go!"

Welles fed her some gas and the car coasted out of the pit area.

Birdy punched the side of the car in frustration as they slowly gained more speed. "Thompson bastards! We're running a hell of a fine race and they're going to try and turn this into a goddamned demolition derby."

As soon as Welles hit the track, he shifted into higher gear and floored it. "I won't let that happen."

● ● ●

It was the final third of the race. In boxing, they called this part of the competition the championship rounds, where everything that had happened before was over and every car on the track would do anything they could do to win. Only now, there was an added bonus for them: take out Jericho Welles and earn a pay day.

It would be an appealing offer even in the best of times. With a depression on, it was manna from heaven. Even drivers who knew they'd finish out of the money might walk away with folding money in their pockets. It was good for them. Bad for Welles.

Welles found himself in dead last place when he coasted back onto the track. Fifteen cars sprawled out along the track in front of him. And deep in his heart, where it counted, he knew he was faster and better than every single one of them. Carter Thompson and his father's money included.

From the start, Welles could see that word of Thompson's bounty had spread among the drivers. The pack bringing up the rear were a hell of a lot more aggressive toward him this time around. The last car at the tail end of the pack eased over towards the right to try to cut him off as he went around the first turn.

Welles saw it coming and slid the car down toward the left and easily shot right past him. One down. Fourteen more to go.

A second pack of five cars were about half way up the straightaway in a tight bunched formation. He figured they'd scatter like balls on a billiard table once he got close and try to block him from passing them.

Birdy knew it, too and called out: "They're in a bunch now, but they're going to separate when you get there. They'll be a bit wobbly when they break formation and start hitting their own headwinds. You should shoot for the gaps where you see them."

Welles shifted into higher gear and floored it on the straightaway, coming on strong as they went into the turn. He eased up on the gas a bit, letting the flock of automobiles pull him along behind him. Just like he knew they would.

The rear car in front of him on his left side wobbled a bit out of the turn, slowing up just enough for Welles to slip in front of him.

The rest of the group packed in tight around Welles at the straightaway; with cars in front of him, behind him and at his side. It was a formation that drivers called 'The Rocking Chair'. They thought they had boxed him in.

They were wrong.

Welles held position until the next turn, when their natural momentum took them higher to the right side of the track. Welles knew his car had superior handling and fought the wheel and his own momentum to keep to the left.

He edged out toward the left just enough to once again sling shot past the car in front of him and coast past the rest of the flock.

He'd gotten out of the rocking chair and found himself in ninth place on the straightaway. He put her into higher gear again and found himself gaining nicely on the eight car.

The eighth car was all alone, trailing the seventh car by a good half of the straightaway.

Welles fed her more gas again and caught up fast. The driver slid over to the left to try to block his path but misjudged the motion and wound up skidding wild on the grass, spinning out to a dead stop.

Welles now had sole position of eighth place and was gaining on seventh.

The seventh place car tried to do the same thing, but fishtailed and missed just as badly.

By now, Welles could hear the roar of the crowd as he took the seventh spot and showed no signs of slowing down. He had a nice view of the field laid out before him on the straightaway. A group of four cars were packed in another tight formation just ahead of him.

And in front of them, Milano and Carter were battling it out for first place as their cars careened around the track.

"Watch these bastards in the turn, Champ," Birdy called out to him. "If they're in on the bounty, their pits have probably gotten on the wireless and told them how the last group missed you. They'll be ready for us."

Welles fed her some gas as he flew into the turn. "And we'll be ready for them."

As he got closer to the pack, the group broke formation and went into a wide, checkerboard pattern. There was plenty of space between cars, but not enough for Welles to sneak through.

The tail car hung back and, as Welles tried to pass, slid over into his lane to try to bump his rear tires. He'd anticipated the move and sped up. The rear car narrowly missed his rear wheel in the process.

Welles took the next turn higher than he'd wanted to and one of the cars glided in front to block him as they came out of the turn.

Welles decided to take a gamble. A small opening had opened on his left side between two cars. Not wide enough to pass through, but wider than the other drivers had intended. He banked toward it, forcing the other driver to steer to the left to avoid a crash and bumped into the car next to him. Both cars lost control spun out onto the grass. It gave Welles the opening he needed and he shot forward right between the two cars in front of him.

The crowd roared. Welles was now in third place and showing no signs of slowing down.

Any rush that Welles might've felt was short lived because Birdy called out, "She's running awfully hot, champ, so be gentle with her for a lap or so. That engine will blow if you don't lay off a bit. We've still got a while yet before the finish."

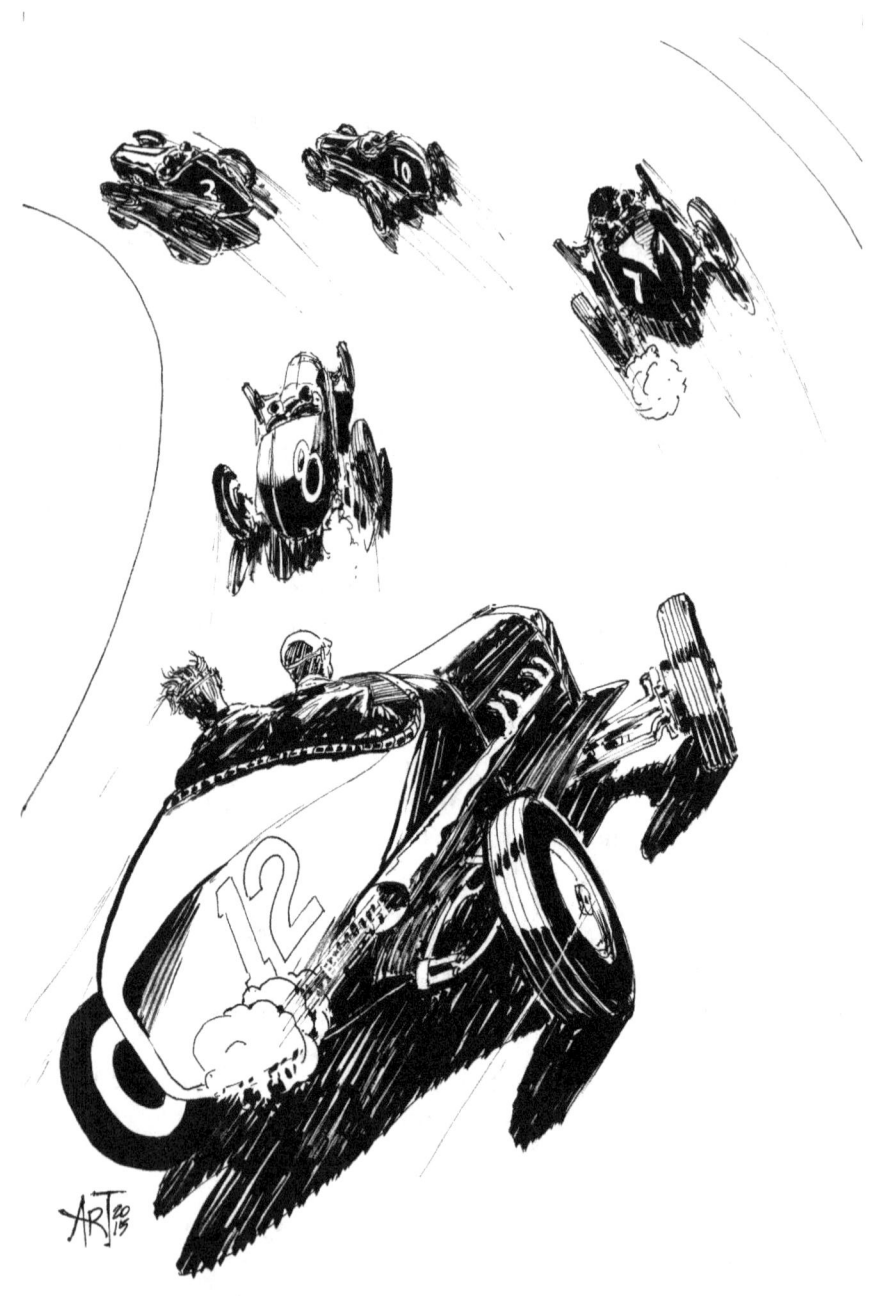

"Watch these bastards in the turn, Champ."

Welles heeded the advice, but he didn't like it. The pack he'd just cleared was now a distant memory as Welles coasted around the track for a couple of laps to let the engine cool for a bit.

He was all alone in a comfortable third while he watched Milano and Carter duke it out for the lead. Each man trying to cut off the other to maintain position. First Milano, then Carter and back again.

"Looks like one hell of a dog fight between those two," Birdy called out. "Guess no one told Milano that Carter's supposed to win!"

Welles knew it wouldn't matter if they had. Because Milano wasn't the kind of guy who threw a race for anyone. For any reason.

Welles had thought he'd been that kind of guy once. And then Thompson and his goons showed up and waived a lot of money under his nose to take a dive. Sure, he'd needed the money. His wife and kids needed that money and they needed it bad.

But kids needed a father more than anything else. They needed a man who could look them in the eye and tell them right from wrong. They needed a father who could look at himself in the mirror every morning and know he'd always done the best he could by them, win or lose.

Because he knew once you start selling out, you'd keep on selling out until nothing of your former self remained. You just gave up. You settled.

And Jericho Welles wasn't the type of man who settled. He never had been. And he would not start now.

With five laps to go, he threw the engine into high gear, opening her up full and floored it.

The car responded immediately. She sank low as he hit the straightaway, running hotter and faster now than she ever had before. The car came alive. She damned near *flew*.

The wind tore at Welles' face as he heard Birdy yell: "Careful, Jerry, careful! All the gears are kissing red now and you're going to blow her out. You…"

But Welles couldn't hear him any more. His blood was pounding in his ears. All the sweat on his body evaporated and his mouth went dry. Every ounce of who and what he was now existed only existed in his hands and feet.

After all these laps and damned near five hundred miles, he and the car had now finally become one. They anticipated each others moves and desires. Flesh and bone had meshed with gears and grease. It felt as if the car wanted to win just as badly as Welles did. Maybe even more. The car was now an extension of himself.

The gap between him and the two lead cars shrank quickly as he picked up more and more speed. He could hear the men and women of the bandstand cheer wildly for him, even over the roar of his engine.

Jericho Welles was coming on strong. *And fast!* Look at him go!

In front of him, Carter and Milano were still dueling for first as Welles came fast out of the turn.

Carter had slipped in close behind Milano to conserve his fuel slowing the other car just enough for him to dart around him at the turn. Milano did the same, the two cars leapfrogging each other time and time again in a desperate struggle for the lead.

Welles let them, settling in behind them in a lower gear, completing a tight speeding pack as it sped around the course. He played it smart. He bided his time.

●●●

The three lead cars were in a straight line in the home stretch. Milano in the lead and getting everything he could out of his machine to maintain his lead. Carter was right behind him with Welles close in at third.

After the final turn, Carter made his move and slid out of the slipstream to shoot past Milano.

Carter had made his move.

So did Welles.

He used Carter's own momentum to slip past him and bolt into the lead.

Welles threw the car back into high gear and opened her up as wide as she would go. The momentum hurdled him forward. The engine roared as she filled with gas. The crowd cheered loudly as Welles found himself in the lead position for the first time in the entire race.

Birdy was screaming something at him, but Welles couldn't hear him any longer.

A quick glance in the mirror showed Carter gaining strong behind him. The white line raced toward him.

Welles couldn't stop now. He didn't want to.

The car kept going faster. Faster.

A blur that might have been a checkered flag raced past him. The white line disappeared.

And then an explosion of smoke and flame leapt before Welles' eyes. The world spun wildly around him, grass and asphalt and people swirling into a single unidentifiable thing. Cars speed past him as the wheel that had been so responsive, so good to him for five hundred miles abandoned him and became a dead thing in his hands.

The wall was the last thing Jericho Welles saw before the whole world went black.

•••

The world took its own sweet time returning to Jericho Welles.

When he finally managed to open his eyes, the first thing he saw was a dirty yellow light shining down upon him.

He'd always hoped that heaven would have a bright, radiant white light to warm him as all the angels and saints came out to take him through those pearly gates.

He hoped to Christ he hadn't wound up in the other place.

He blinked hard again and realized he was actually staring up at the yellow light of the garage. He realized that must mean he was laying flat on his back.

He tried to push himself up on his elbows, but an arching pain shot through his chest and straight to his head. He collapsed again with a groan.

"Stay still," said a familiar voice. He realized it was Butch and felt his big hand easing him back flat. "The doc'll be here any minute now. That hard head of yours took a hell of a beating and it looks like you've got a couple of busted ribs thrown in for good measure."

"Birdy," Welles gasped, despite the pain. "What happened to Birdy?"

Then Birdy's smiling, blackened face came into view. "And just who do you think pulled you out of there, you stubborn son of a bitch?"

Welles reached out for him, but the pain shot through his chest again and he stopped. "What...what the hell happened out there?"

"We were running real hot that last lap," Birdy said. "Gauges were all well past red, right off the scale. I tried telling you to settle in behind Carter to keep him from winning, but I guess you didn't hear me."

"I...didn't." All he could remember was how everything was a blur right after he got in front of Carter and before he hit the wall.

Butch held a glass to his mouth and fed him some water. His gagged as it went down. His throat felt raw, almost burned, but the water made him feel a bit clearer. "Did...did we win?"

Butch and Birdy looked at each other before they hoisted up a large silver cup from beneath the table where Welles was laying. They didn't have to say anything. Seeing that trophy and the looks on their faces said it all.

"Milano came in second," Birdy smiled. "Catapulted around Carter just like you did at the last minute. Carter came in a close third, but third just the same."

Welles shut his eyes and felt water streaming down the side of his face. He didn't know if Butch had doused him with water again or if they were his own tears. He was betting on the latter.

"Old Man Thompson's gonna be mighty steamed," Birdy said. "His boy coming in second is bad enough, but third'll probably damned near kill him."

Welles heard a door slam open somewhere in the garage, followed by a lot of commotion. He was too sore to move, but it sounded like a lot of people had just piled into the room in a great big hurry. Reporters, he thought, and adoring fans maybe all looking to see how the champ was doing.

Jericho Welles. Racing Champion. He sure did like the sound of that.

He didn't like the sound he heard next.

"Let me at that dirty, double-crossing, no good hillbilly son of a bitch," Old Man Thompson yelled. "I had a deal with that miserable shitkicker. Who the hell does he think he is?"

Welles didn't have the strength to open his eyes, but he heard himself say: "I know who I am. The winner of the..."

Another scuffle broke out. Shouting and scuffling of feet that sounded like men shoving each other.

And then Welles heard something that he hadn't heard in a very long time. A metallic click that could only come from someone thumbing back the hammer on a gun. Then he heard another.

Despite the pain, Welles lifted his head and looked at what was happening around him. Old Man Thompson was holding a gun on Butch. So were the three goons Thompson had brought with him.

And Butch was aiming a gun at Thompson.

"Think it over, old man," Butch told him. "Anything happens, you get it first. Right between your beady little eyes."

Thompson's ruddy face got even redder. "Of all the gall! You're out gunned and out manned."

But Butch didn't budge. "And you're dead if you and your boys don't lay those guns on the floor. Right now."

At first, Welles didn't know if the pain or the shot he'd taken to the head was making him hear things, but he could've sworn he heard someone clapping.

But judging by the way the others reacted, it looked like they'd all heard it, too.

And that's when Welles saw Archie Doyle walked through bay doors of the garage, applauding like he'd just seen the last act of one of those Broadway shows he used to put on.

"Damned impressive, Billy," Doyle said to Thompson. "Since when did you scrounge up enough money to walk around with hired goons like that?"

Welles didn't know if Thompson realized he was lowering his gun, but he was lowering it anyway. So did the three men with him. "Why…Archie. These men are old friends of mine, see? Men who bet on my son to win the race."

"Friends of yours?" Doyle pulled out a cigar and took his time lighting it. When he got a good burn going, he said, "Since when do you have any friends?"

But Thompson was in no mood for ribbing, not even from Doyle. "Knock it off, will you, Archie? This punk cost me a hell of a lot of money. This is serious business I've got going on here."

Doyle squinted at him through the cigar smoke. "Damned right it's serious. Because judging by the way these clowns are dressed, I'd say they're not from around here, are they?" He made a show of looking at the three men, then said: "Nope. Those look like city threads to me and not from Cleveland and certainly not from Indianapolis. I'd say those are Detroit suits." His grin disappeared. "Or Chicago."

Thompson's face turned a pinker shade of red damned fast. "Now just wait a minute, Archie. You…"

"I've been waitin' a lot of minutes, Billy. A lot of minutes since I heard you've been workin' awfully hard to cozy up to Capone's old outfit up in Chicago. Tryin' to open up your own channels to sell that panther piss you peddle as moonshine. I heard you were plannin' on usin' your winnings from today's race to bankroll your new channel. More stills. More trucks. And more drivers for them trucks."

"Now just hold on a minute, Archie. I…"

Doyle motioned to Thompson's gun with his cigar. "How about puttin' that thing away before you try talkin' yourself out of this one?"

Thompson looked down at the revolver, then at the three men with him. They hadn't put their guns away either. And as he looked back at Doyle, Welles saw a thought appear behind Thompson's eyes.

He knew Doyle must've seen it too because the man from Five Points grew very still. Not still the way some men get when they're scared. Still the way some men get when they're about to go wild. "I said put it down, Billy, before I take it away from you."

Thompson swallowed hard before he slowly laid the gun on the floor. His popping knees from the effort were the only sound in the silent garage.

None of the three goons from Chicago moved.

Doyle said, "That goes for you ladies, too. Or I tell Nitti all about the shit you boys tried to pull here today."

All three laid their guns on the floor and stepped back from them.

Doyle looked at Butch, who still hadn't lowered his gun. "You look like a pro."

Butch stood a little taller from the compliment. "Because I am."

"Good. Keep them covered. This won't last too long."

Thompson began to shake as Doyle slowly walked toward him. "Damn it, Archie. I've got a damned nice operation here."

"Damned right you do. I'm the one who gave it to you, remember? Gave you the Cleveland route. Parts of Philly. Even clear on out to Detroit."

"But Chicago…"

Welles flinched when Doyle slapped Thompson hard across the mouth. It wasn't a punch, but the hardest slap he'd ever seen a grown man take. "Chicago is out of your league, stupid. And the only reason why I let you stay in this business this long is because you've got a freight hauling company and a couple of stills in the boonies. You only run my booze because I tell you to run my booze the way I want you to run it."

Then, he pointed back at the Chicago goons. "You know what these bastards would've done to you? They'd strip you clean a month after you threw in with them without me backing you. They would've taken your trucks and your hooch and then were does that leave me? Havin' to go to Chicago, hat in hand just to get back a quarter of what's already mine. And all because you decided to play gangster."

"But Archie, I…"

"Yeah, I know. They promised you the world. Told you how you could get along just fine without me. That there was no way I'd ever find out about it." He leaned in closer to Thompson. "But I did find out about it, didn't I?"

Thompson pulled his head back and Archie slapped him again. "Didn't I?"

Thompson surprised Welles when the old man began to cry. "Yes, Archie. Yes, you did."

He snatched Thompson by the tie and pulled him closer. "And it's a good thing for you I did. Because when I'd found out about it after they'd ripped you off, you would've been better off if they'd killed you in the bargain because I'd make you hurt for a long time before I let you die."

He released Thompson with a shove, then looked at the three goons. "You boys better beat it back to Chicago on the PDQ and see Nitti first thing. And a word of advice: If you're smart, you'll go into his office on your knees. He ain't too happy with any of you nitwits right now."

None of the three men tried to pick up their guns as they filed out the door.

Thompson was left all by himself, alone and blubbering in the middle of the garage. Beaten, broke and all alone.

Doyle motioned for Butch to put his gun away and he did.

Doyle circled Thompson slowly, the way Welles had seen wild dogs circle a wounded animal before attacking. "You're ruined, Billy. You know it and I know it. You made a play for the big time and you failed because you're not the big time. I am. I've been doing this my whole life and I don't know how to do nothin' else. And the only reason why I'm gonna let you walk out of here is because you didn't steal anythin' from me. You're just stupid, that's all and you're lucky that I think people can learn from bein' stupid."

He shoved Thompson toward the door. "Now get the hell out of here and go home. I'll be by to see you before I leave town. And if you're not there when I come callin', you'll be sorry when I find you."

Thompson didn't bother to pick up his hat or his gun or straighten out his tie as he trudged out of the garage. The gun and busted carnation were the only evidence he'd been there at all.

When Doyle turned to face Welles, he was all smiles again, like nothing had even happened. "How you holdin' up, kid?"

Welles let his head drop back onto the table. "You going to work me over, too?"

Doyle laughed. "Are you kiddin'? After what you just did out there? I don't think I could take you, even with you flat on your back like this."

He looked at Butch. "You in the market for four heaters?"

Butch smiled. "Always, Mr. Doyle."

He nodded toward the guns on the floor. "Then take 'em as a bonus. Compliments of the house on a job well done. Then give us the room, will ya, kid? I've got to talk to the champ here."

Butch scooped up the weapons and walked out through the garage door.

Welles nodded to Birdy and said, "He stays. Anything you've got to say to me, you can say in front of him."

Doyle shrugged. "No skin off my nose." He reached in his pocket and laid the mortgage on Welles' chest. "There's your mortgage, just like I promised. Marked paid in full and signed by me this very day. You earned it."

"You're goddamned right I did," Welles said before finally letting himself pass out.

The End

The Checkered Flag

Every story I've ever written is linked to all those that have come before it. My westerns, my 1930s stories, my modern day spy thrillers and my science fiction all take place in the same universe. I do this on purpose. It makes it fun to write and, I hope, fun for the audience to read.

THE RACER'S EDGE is an off-shoot of the story that begins in FIGHT CARD: AGAINST THE ROPES and continues in PROHIBITION and several short stories, where the lives of so many people are affected by one man—Archie Doyle.

Some writers enjoy telling a new story every time they sit at the keyboard. They're able to spin unique tales that take the reader in a new direction each time. I envy them. My mind doesn't work that way. It would be easier if it did. Instead, I seek to add to the world I've created in my earlier works: populating it with new characters who are anchored in the same frame of reference. For me, every story is like a ripple in a lake. Each story has some effect on the universe I have created.

Archie Doyle may be a supporting character in that universe, but he's certainly an important one. He is a victim and profiteer of the changing times of which I write. He is a product of the Prohibition Era; that glorious time in American history where well-meaning people thought banning vice was the right thing to do. But instead of stopping drinking, they spurred the eventual creation of a criminal empire that spanned the nation; the remnants of which remain to this day.

Archie Doyle didn't create Prohibition, but he certainly profited from it. Until alcohol was banned by the federal government, he was nothing more than a street criminal. A neighborhood thug who had more brains than most, but not many prospects. After the Volstead Act passed, Doyle and men like him became barons of booze. They were willing to break the law to give people what they wanted. This gave them power.

THE RACER'S EDGE is very much part of that saga, where we see a former driver within the Doyle operation trying to go straight, but can't quite escape his past. It is his desire to remake himself that spurs him to change his life and – ultimately – win security for himself and his family. May all of us be so lucky. I sincerely hope you enjoyed my story and will consider reading some of my other works.

●●●

TERRENCE P. McCAULEY - is an award-winning writer of crime fiction. His first techno-thriller, SYMPATHY FOR THE DEVIL, was published by Polis Books in July 2015. Polis also republished Terrence's first two novels set in 1930 New York City – PROHIBITION and SLOW BURN. Terrence has had short stories featured in Thuglit, Spinetingler Magazine, Shotgun Honey, Big Pulp and other publications. He is a member of the New York City chapter of the Mystery Writers of America, the International Thriller Writers and the International Crime Writers Association. A proud native of The Bronx, NY, he is currently writing his next work of fiction. Terrence is represented by Doug Grad of the Doug Grad Literary Agency.

FOURTH
AND INCHES
by
J. Walt Layne

August 19, 1938

*I*t'll be a thrill a minute with your man Tim Hill. Live from South Bend *and abroad with the Fighting Irish. As KSBI and the National Broadcasting Company, bring you another fine season of collegiate athletics. Our distinguished guest later in the hour will be none other than Notre Dame's own head coach Emmett Layton and his star linebacker, the Old Hardhead, Harper 'Jack' Hull. Stay tuned during this short break from the Machinist's Co-op.*

It was the first football practice of the season. Coach Emmett Layton had gotten special permission for the football squad to return to campus a full month early in order to hone their skills. Not that he felt they needed it, but because the nature of the game was about to drastically change. He hadn't known that KSBI was coming, or the loaded question he was about to be asked.

We're back in South Bend at the Home of the Irish. Head Coach Layton is with us, along with his pile driving sophomore lineman, the Old Hardhead Jack Hull, to talk about what lies ahead. Coach, can the fans and followers of the pride of South Bend expect more of the same from your powerhouse line and the sure shot arm of quarterback Tom Reese. I thought we'd get the coach's take on the Collegiate Athletics Board's decision to integrate American College and University Football schedules with that of the Negro colleges.

This was the first question that caught Layton flat-footed, "Well Tim as you know it is a change for sure. We at Notre Dame will run the program which has served us well and will preserve Coach Rockne's legacy."

Then the little radioman turned to Hull, and the words that came out of his mouth changed Notre Dame Football forever.

No trepidation here to be found in South Bend, I turn now to Lineman Jack Hull, whose flawless play helped lead the Irish to a 9-1 season closing on another national title in 1937. Jack how do you see you and your brethren of the gridiron faring in your season opener, the exhibition scrimmage against the Morehouse Tigers, the pride of the Negro college system?

The question hung there between the three of them. Tim Hill looked sheepish after having asked a cheap and loaded question. Layton's angry look shifted from Hill to Jack Hull who towered a foot over Layton, and 18 inches plus one hundred fifty pounds over Hill who might soon be the late voice of the Irish.

Hull's predatory eyes narrowed and focused on the little man. Layton put his six-foot, two hundred pound chassis between the Mississippi Madman and the mouthpiece just in time. Hull brushed Layton aside on his way to the door. Just as Layton was extolling the merits of the cheap question Hull growled, "I reckon we'll just see."

Tim Hill started after Hull, but Layton jerked him back, upsetting the RCA 44B microphone. Layton glared down at the meek Hill and growled, "That was a cheap shot, even for the likes of you, Timmy. If I see you around here before the bus leaves for Atlanta, I'm gonna let Jack Hull lay one on you, and then I'm gonna tell that Shirley Temple you run like a rutting buck all about it."

•••

"When in the hell were you planning to tell me?" Layton thundered over the desk at the Director of Athletics for Notre Dame, George McGhee.

McGhee cringed, and then spoke quietly. "The board and I appreciate your anger Emmett. But the governing body of the university felt differently. The other schools in the Ivy League have already embraced the notion that the best way to maintain our status is to settle once and for all the question of whether or not the athletes in these black colleges are even good enough to compete with our boys."

Layton frowned, "When was the decision made?"

"They decided last fall, when the Morehouse team completed their third perfect season. They didn't tell me until the end of the spring term. I didn't tell you because..."

Layton fixed his eyes on McGhee, who met his gaze momentarily and then looked away, as Layton said, "Well?"

McGhee averted his eyes and then looked back to Layton, "Well because I knew we'd be having this discussion and frankly, I didn't want to you to resign and put me in the position to have to explain why you left to the board and a new head coach."

Layton was seething, "Leave, hell. We're goin' to Morehouse to reckon with that mess and put a halt to this inter-league business once and for all."

McGhee ran a hand over his face and stood up. He walked to the window and looked down on the field where the gathering players were going over fundamental drill with their squad captains. "Emmett, I'm afraid there's more to it than that. According to our schedules, The College Athletics Board wants to give them their own conference."

"Never you mind about that. I have a legacy to preserve here, the parents of the team and the supporters don't buy on new fangled ideas. They want titles and traditions and look to me to get it done and I, by God, am going to get it done. But when the season closes at the end of October, you get that bunch of cigar smoking, brandy swilling, elbow rubbing jackasses together to accept my resignation and I'm going back to Alabama." Layton growled.

"Is that all this is about, that the Morehouse players happen to be colored?" McGhee asked, in a poor rooted attempt to change the subject.

"I wouldn't care any less about the color of their skin if they were lime green like those radar men from Mars. I am not going to answer questions from families about what if my boy catches something playing football with a bunch of…"

McGhee wheeled and held up a hand, cutting him off clean. "I get it Emmett, and direct any of your family problems through me. I'll tell them how it'll be if their sons want to play for the Irish."

"I don't direct problems other places, I take care of them myself. Is there anything else George? I have a practice to run." Layton cut him of just as cleanly.

"Yes, two things. First, it's an exhibition scrimmage, it doesn't count. You'll play four five-minute periods. Second, Emmett I understand you threatened the radio fellow from the local station. That Tim Hill kid, his daddy who owns the station called."

"I tell you what, you have any trouble with him, you tell him to call me. I'll straighten him out on asking cheap shot questions just to break a news story. Sensationalism isn't going to catch on any more than your Interconference football." Layton growled.

"All right Emmett, I'll see you in twelve weeks. In the mean time try to remember that you're here to win titles not re-fight the Civil War," McGhee said, the timid edge leaving his voice as his words clattered against the slamming door.

That afternoon after an unmerciful but brief pep talk, Layton bypassed the usual cobweb dusting of first practices and ran the boys in a full-bore drill that nearly retired the prep team. At closing time, the steam room in the gym still held nineteen weary bodies, none of whom would report to the first team.

● ● ●

The following afternoon in Atlanta, Georgia, Harvey T. Burwell was sitting down to lunch in the small eat-in kitchen of his home less than a mile from Morehouse Stadium. His wife Mavis had hastily prepared a simple meal of fried eggs and grits, his being home on a Friday afternoon was out of the ordinary, as was his excuse, "I need a little time to work on a sermon and get a test ready."

The radio was already on and tuned to the National Broadcasting Company's local affiliate, WAGR when Mavis brought the plate to the table. The announcer opened with, "And now its time for syndicated sports news from around the nation." Mavis smiled at him and said, "A sermon I could have believed. But a test two weeks before camp begins or students arrive, you got to work on that one Harvey T."

He shushed her as the announcer launched into a rapid fire report on sports around the nation. He hammed through the statistics for a baseballer from the Brooklyn Dodgers. Mavis left the kitchen to gather her purse and the broadcaster segued into the college scouting and preseason reporting when she returned to the kitchen to kiss his cheek and announce her departure for a ladies circle meeting. But she pulled up short when the announcer said—

Where UGA failed to deliver last season, Coach Harvey Burwell's Morehouse College Tiger's will have their go at the Fighting Irish. On September 9 the Morehouse College Stadium will host Coach Layton's boys from South Bend in an exhibition scrimmage to inaugurate and welcome Burwell and Morehouse to the American College Athletics Association. Stay tuned in the weeks ahead for updates on what is certain to be a widely talked about event as the best of colored college football hosts the pride of America.

"Did he just say...?" Harvey asked Mavis, nearly choking on a fork loaded with grits and eggs.

"No, Sir, he said it twice." She said quietly, tears welling in her eyes. Mavis knew that her Harvey, despite academics, secretly harbored the desire to see his boys excel beyond the limit of the designation 'colored.'

"I have to get back to the office. We got to get these boys in. Why didn't I know anything about this? That's four weeks from now, why do I always hear stuff last when it affects me first?" Harvey said, standing up quickly.

"Harvey Burwell, you better not waste that dinner when you know I'm trying to get out of here to go to my ladies circle meeting. That football will be there when you get back."

Harvey lifted the plate from the table, giving her a sidelong glance, as if he were her child and not her husband, "But, Mave." He said, raking the last of the food on the plate into a pile and into his open mouth. "My… My boys is finally gonna get their chance."

"Well God bless them, but you Harvey T. have got to work on your table manners." She laughed and kissed his cheek as he donned his hat and headed for the door.

When the newspapers caught wind of the story and the phones started ringing for interviews, Coach Burwell made the decision to close his training camp so that prying, distracting, and well-meaning eyes alike would not provide any unnecessary distraction. Daily, the number of phone calls increased. Some were reporters, others supporters, the worst were the ones that came late at night to his home. The ignorance of the common person was more socially accepted in the south, unless you were the victim.

Late Thursday night the following week, Coach Burwell was leaving the stadium after a very long day. He was nearly to his car when he heard a car door open and close. Burwell wasn't a small man by any means, but after the recent threats it would have been foolhardy not to be a little afraid.

He heard hard soled shoes on the gravel and was ready to strike when the boyish face of Atlanta Beacon sports reporter Stephen Queryl Jones appeared rounding the dark corner of the Model A. Burwell nearly had a heart attack.

"Coach Burwell, Stephen Q. Jones with the Atlanta Beacon," the kid said quickly.

"I recognize you Squirrelly, what are you doin' out here in the dark scaring the bejeezus out of folks?"

"Well I'd have come inside, but…" the reporter started.

"But what?" Burwell went on the defensive.

"Well for one, you've closed training camp. Secondly, the Beacon has not had an overly friendly relationship with your community, so I didn't know if you'd talk to me." The young reporter said very candidly.

"My community? I'd say you have a pretty good idea why that is. Nobody cared about my Tigers when we won four football titles, four baseball titles, and eleven basketball titles when I was coaching full time. Nowadays with this depression on, and we're lucky to have enough boys for a team at all no body cared. But suddenly the College Athletics Board wants to integrate so they can appear like a progressive organization and WAGR replays an interview some radio jaw-jacker did with Coach Layton up there at Notre Dame, and suddenly my stadium, on my time with my boys is suddenly everybody's business. You tell me why that is, and I might take an interest in letting you into MY community. No need to come around here looking for a story." Burwell growled, venting pressure.

"Coach, coach, coach… I am not here to start a fight. If you haven't read or heard the things being said in the coffee shops and country clubs around this country, you will soon. I am looking for a story, but I'm here to help. Everybody in this country including Denver Smith, my editor-in-chief, and owner of the Beacon says this is just another way to take away something wholly owned by the clean shirt crowd and give it over to a bunch of heatherns."

"You do know there's no 'r' in heathen?" Burwell said, showing more concern for the man's pronunciation of the words, than what they meant.

"Not accordin' to my Granny."

Burwell grinned, "All right, for the sake of your Granny, tell me what's on your mind."

●●●

'Burwell's Tigers to Host Irish Hooligans,' the headline of the Atlanta Beacon glared ominously from the center post of the sled. Jack Hull shouldered into the center post onto which the newspaper had been strapped to the pad with such force that assistant coach Roy Meeks was literally thrown clear of the sled as it broke loose.

The ferocious sound of Coach Layton's relentless driving of the squads through calisthenics and timed relays harkened to his days as a Marine Corps trainee in the 1920s. The offense and defense broke into thirds to run plays, and Layton pressed on, crossing the name of any player not giving his all off the list.

●●●

Saturday September 10, 1938

It was a typical hot late summer day in Atlanta, Georgia. Morehouse College Stadium filled. Today's game was like no other before it. On this day, Coach Emmett Layton and the Notre Dame Fighting Irish had come to town to play an exhibition scrimmage with Coach Harvey Burwell's Morehouse Tigers.

The coaches were giving their benches a final pep talk and the players were focused on the task after the turn over. Each man glared across the no man's land that was the gridiron trying to intimidate his unknown opponent.

The stadium wasn't designed with segregation in mind, but today the HOME side of the field was nearly all black. The few exceptions were the dozen police officers, a few fence roosters, and the gang in the press box. The VISITOR side was nearly all white with the exception of attendants and custodians, and other stadium staff and employees who happened to draw the short straw that day and had their own fence rooters to contend with.

The din of the crowds and the competing announcers made it difficult to hear the young vendors calling out. A kid selling programs in the upper bent of the visitor's stands tripped over his own feet and had it not been for the lightning hand of a policeman, he would have likely tumbled all the way to the ground level, one concrete step at a time.

●●●

Sweat poured from the scalp of Morehouse Center, Clevin Mayes, and ran down his forehead. Were it not for his furrowed brow channeling the rivulets along either side of his wide brown nose the stinging salt would have blinded him.

"Twins, thirty two, shuttle, Hike!" the quarterback, Roosevelt King called out, and Mayes shot the ball between his knees.

Mayes didn't usually look to see if King got it. He always got it. If he didn't get it, the referee would call it dead once it hit the ground. But for some reason, be it the sun, or the opposing line of big angry white faces, or late adolescent angst, Mayes took his eyes off the behemoth bull of a man in front of him for a split second to lower his head and follow the ball as it arced toward King's outstretched, waiting hands.

●●●

Jack Hull's knuckles were white, his weight forward. He waited for the snap, beyond the quarterback's jabbering play call. He didn't know the home team's playbook, but he knew enough football to know the cadence of the game. The first play of the game after kickoff and return would be a passing play.

He watched the dark hand of the center grip the red brown leather ball. He sneered and growled at the smaller man trying to intimidate him. Hull didn't call names and jeer, he was there for football, he'd been taught better, and it meant something to him.

Hull couldn't believe what he was seeing. The quarterback called the play, and after the Center hiked the ball, he lowered his head to watch the ball sail to the quarterback. Hull seized the moment, as the ball and the center's head went into motion so did he.

Hull's legs fired and three hundred fifteen pounds of Mississippi Madman shot forward across the line of scrimmage. He pressed a hand down on the back of the bent over Center driving the man to the ground as he rocketed past. He saw the quarterback catch the ball from the Center and drop back, scanning for a receiver.

●●●

Quarterback Roosevelt King grabbed the ball out of the air as if in slow motion. He shuffled back two steps and scanned for either of the two receivers he expected to be open. He thought he'd seen the Center look underneath to follow the ball, he prayed that he was wrong. He realized when he cocked his arm to throw to the outstretched and open hands thirty yards down field that the foreground was filled with the giant linebacker that the papers called The Old Hardhead.

The lights went out momentarily when Hull slammed into King like a freight train, driving him up and back ten feet before slamming him down to earth, "Welcome to the A.C. Double A!" The vicious face growled as King opened his eyes.

●●●

On the field, Morehouse's first series of plays were over. The coaches were silent and going over their clipboard lists for any forgotten until the last minute details.

Coach Layton signaled to Notre Dame Quarterback Tim Reese as the Irish huddled a dozen feet from where the referee spotted the ball. Reese explained the strong side split buck pass play and the huddle broke.

The Irish took the line and the Tigers lined up in an unfamiliar manned coverage formation with a tall stocky Back named Carboy deep.

Reese called the play; Hull, who was playing Center, hiked the ball. As the play unfolded the Ends and Guards blocked. Hull grabbed both tackles and plowed them back a dozen feet. Reese, with all the time in the world waited for the Tight Ends to reach the zenith of their routes. As the strong side of coverage began to collapse, he turned on his heel and fired the ball to Marcum, the open weak side Tight End.

The ball whizzed between two encroaching tackles and into Marcum's waiting hands. He turned and ran with the ball racing toward the end zone forty yards distant. As the two tackles diverged from their collision course with each other, and were hot on his tail.

"Reese has all day and fires the ball to Marcum. Marcum's got it and heads for the end zone. Morehouse tackles Carrithers and Jones is after him. It's Marcum at the thirty, the twenty..."

Marcum's chest was on fire as he pumped his legs and ran as fast as he could for the end zone. He heard boots tearing up the grass behind him and the easy breathing of a man in much better shape. He knew he was had before he felt the man's arms close around him.

"Carrithers closes the distance between himself, and the ball carrier. Morehouse freshman Cedric Carrithers brings down Marcum at the fifteen." The voice of WAGR radio, Avery Reed buzzed from the loudspeakers. The crowd on the VISTORS side of the stadium booed and hissed, while the HOME side cheered.

Carrithers pushed himself up and looked down at the shaken Marcum. He offered a hand. Marcum looked at the hand for a long moment and the stadium was suddenly silent. Marcum hadn't known what to expect and a gesture of kindness from such a dark countenance was unexpected.

"Gonna just let me hang, with all these people watching?" Carrithers asked shaking his hand to be sure Marcum saw it.

Marcum frowned at the graveled voice and took the hand, "Just unexpected."

"This is a university. We're black, not ignorant.' Carrithers grunted as he pulled Marcum up.

"You're pretty fast," Marcum said as he walked off.

"Not really, you just run like a chicken." The stout tackle grunted.

Avery Reed's play by play coverage continued, "There will be a momentary break as the officials spot the ball at center field. Morehouse stopped the run in the Visitor's side belt after a 22-yard advance. I'd have liked to hear the exchange between Marcum and Carrithers. "

•••

On both sides of the field as Marcum and Carrithers returned to their respective benches Coach Burwell and Harvey asked almost simultaneously, "What was that about?"

"I ate the ground and he was giving me a hand up," Marcum replied.

"He didn't know what to expect 'cause he never played football with a black man before." Carrithers said as he raised a ladle of water from the bucket.

Burwell subbed in two of his smallest linebackers for the tackles, growling into the last one's ear, "Look for a hole, sack that quarterback. They want to make a pitch and score early to make a show."

Layton gave Reese the baseball hand signal for a fastball, telling him to throw the heater, a short fast pass to the first tight end to break the line and get open. Reese gave him the nod. In any other game, Reese might have questioned Layton's judgment, back to back forward passing plays was a good way to tip the other team to your strategy. Reese was from a small high school in Vermont that won many games on changeup trick plays built out of three modifications of one formation. He liked to keep it moving.

"They're lined up on the fifteen. Hull's set, Reese calls and there's the hike." Avery announced as Hull snapped the ball.

A split second before the ball left the ground there was movement in Hull's periphery. He snapped the ball a bit hard and Reese tipped it. The ball shot straight upwards off Reese's fingers, and both men swore to themselves as Avery Reed announced to America.

"Notre Dame ball on the Morehouse fifteen, there's the snap. It looks like a pop fly as Reese tips it. Morehouse in motion as it falls fair, Reese tries to recover, play ruled dead at the seventeen. The Irish lose two on that one, Layton sends in a new play along with instructions for Hull and Reese to stick with football." Reed quipped, and the crowd to roared.

Reese nodded to the sideline, but aside from Layton's shaking finger, he got no signal. He and Hull exchanged a look and a nod as they lined up on the Seventeen. Reese called the slant change up he was known for and Hull snapped the ball.

As it came he caught it clean, side dressed as the lines clashed, and rolled backward. Straight ahead Hull crashed through the line like a Viking berserker. He was free, clear of the line, and chugged onward another ten yards before he turned and looked.

As Reese cocked and threw, both of Morehouse's small linebackers broke the line and rushed, but the ball was already away.

Downfield, the ball made a straight cut through traffic, just above head height of the clashing lines. Hull caught the ball on the five and ran it into the end zone unopposed.

"That's six for the Irish, and the point after makes seven. The official sets the ball on the tee, and Mortenson sends it away. Carrithers takes it on the bounce at the ten and…"

•••

Carrithers signaled two kibitzing teammates to pay attention. Mortenson's boot contacting the ball sounded like a shot. Carrithers fixed his eyes on the ball and stepped up as it came in. The ball came to earth a bit more sharply than he anticipated. He backpedaled and made an awkward hugging catch. He pulled the ball in and corrected his hold on it as he ran down field.

He had no trouble weaving his way through the initial wave of green sweaters and saw the field opening up in front of him. He bobbed left and rolled his shoulder beneath a pair of tackling arms. Carrithers glanced back for a split second, not believing he'd slipped the tackle, and as he turned his head forward to look down field, the lights went out.

"Carrithers brought to a halt just north of midfield, blindsided by McGinn." Avery Reed announced, followed by, "And there's the timekeeper's bell and that will signal the end of the first period of play in this truncated exhibition. Those of you listening at home, please stay with us during these brief announcements."

Carrithers was slow getting to his knees after the hit, and McGinn just stood there, taunting him. He pushed himself up to his knees and slowly recovered to his feet. As his bell stopped ringing and his eyes focused on the big Irishman, Carrithers focused on what he was saying.

McGinn stood there berating the dazed Carrithers and was surprised as recognition suddenly returned to his face and the smaller man launched himself, just as two of his teammates caught him and ushered him off the field.

Layton met McGinn on his way back to the bench, "What's got into

He saw the field opening up in front of him.

you, you lunkhead? You hit that man full bore, and you bait him to fight? How about you ride the bench awhile?"

McGinn sneered at him, "Coach!"

Layton squared up in front of the bigger man, "What?"

McGinn sneered again, "Nothin'."

Layton jabbed a finger from McGinn to the bench and the whirled to the waiting second team, "Russell get in there. You just made the first team!" He glared at McGinn.

● ● ●

"One minute remains in the second period of play and King breaks the huddle and the Tigers line up in front of an increasingly hostile presence from the Irish." Avery Reed announced as the Tigers mechanically filed to their positions.

The Tigers' Center Clevin Mayes grabbed the ball and King gave the count. Mayes snapped the ball and was instantly head to head with the larger Hull. The old hard head easily folded Mayes out of the way and again engaged and planted Quarterback Roosevelt King before he could get rid of the ball.

"King sacked again, the line of scrimmage will move back to where Hull spotted the Morehouse quarterback and the Tigers will try it again," Reed exhaled along with the crowd.

King's ears buzzed and the heat of embarrassment burned down the back of his neck causing the wool sweater he was wearing to itch. The disheartened din of the crowd tore at him. He glanced at the sideline and caught the signal for another pass, but there was no way he was going to take another ride to the earth.

"Twenty one, twenty one side car shuffle on me," he barked in the huddle. They broke and lined up.

The Irish line looked as impenetrable as it had consistently throughout the game. The Tigers were quickly learning that the Notre Dame team played a different brand of ball than they were used to.

Clevin Mayes bent low and gripped the ball. King surveyed the line and called the play. Mayes snapped the ball, stepped back, turned, and took off like a shot for the sideline as the two guards on either side of him closed the hole and rushed Hull.

As the line closed, King fired the ball to Mayes as he cleared the end of the line and entered the side belt. Mayes caught it on the run and was well on his way to the end zone. He ran unmolested into the end zone and turned around just as the clock hit zero and the buzzer sounded. The score counted according to the board, but all eyes were on the line of scrimmage, where offense and defense had become a brawl.

Mayes dropped the ball, took off his leather helmet, and walked toward the Morehouse bench. He sat alone to watch as Coach Burwell, and the defensive squad ran to assist the Irish offense, Coach Layton, and the officials break up the fight.

•••

Layton watched speechless as Mayes snapped the ball and then backpedaled. When the man turned toward the sideline and jogged off, at first he thought the man was injured. Then the line shifted and the two guards not only slammed together shoulder to shoulder, but they powered forward, mitigating Hull's ability to attack the quarterback.

As the rest of the lines engaged, he watched Russell shoot a hand out and grab a helmet strap. He guessed it was then that punches started flying. The fight spread down the line like wildfire and no one noticed that King had passed to Mayes, or that Mayes had turned the corner. He fumed as Mayes entered the end zone and no one noticed, including the officials.

As Layton called out the offense to help him separate the brawl, he saw Burwell doing the same with his defense. Both coaches and their players walked to the fray so that the officials wouldn't get the idea that they were joining the brawl.

Avery Reed, pausing momentarily from his transition to calling the game like a boxing match said, "At this point the only legal Morehouse player on the field not participating in this fray is Quarterback Roosevelt King. Likewise, the only representative of the Irish not currently ensconced in this football exhibition turned pugilism is Jack Hull. The coaches are bringing assistance to break this one up, and its half time, here in Atlanta".

Layton and Burwell made fast work of sorting out their brawlers, simply grabbing sweaters, green or maroon and yelling, "Go to your bench!" Both coaches were fiercer with their own players than with the others.

Layton and Burwell got to Russell and a Morehouse linebacker named Harris at the same time. Coach Burwell grabbed for Russell's green sweater as he delivered a right handed haymaker to Harris. He wheeled as Burwell hauled him up and cocked a fist.

"Russell," Layton roared and seized him by the chinstrap of his leather helmet and jerked his head around, nose to nose, an inch apart, "Russell, what in the hell has gotten into you?"

Russell stammered and didn't answer.

"That's it, you're done, get on my bench and hold it down!" He led Russell three steps toward the bench.

Layton and Burwell regarded each other momentarily as the last of the players headed for the sidelines. Neither of them spoke, or needed to. Each of them eyed their receding players with anger. They shared a last look and followed their teams.

After ten minutes of ferocious oaths and promises of severe disciplinary action Layton let his team take turns at the water bucket. Burwell did not. He did not berate his team, but reminded them that all eyes were on them, and advised them of expectations and preconceptions.

●●●

"It is hard to believe that these teams have played just ten minutes of football. We have seen it go from a hand extended in a gesture of friendship to a free for all, and then a brawl. I'm not sure at this point if I am coming to you from Morehouse Stadium or ringside. This is Avery Reed with NBC Radio via WAGR."

"Don't pay that any attention," McGinn growled to Marcum as Coach Layton paced back and forth reinforcing his promise to end the football career of any man setting a toe out of line when play resumed.

Layton pounced like a hunting tiger. He was in McGinn's face so fast that the linebacker fell backward off the bench trying to backpedal. "You damned well better pay it a lot of attention. If you're going to play football for the Irish, behaving like some kind of backward ignorant mob will get you sent home in a hurry."

Across the field Coach Harvey Burwell had moved on from the brawl, "You all have to get that line tight, and I mean solid like a dam. And when the defense lines up, I want all you smaller, faster guys out there. Carrithers, you gonna play in both directions. Roundtree, you play both sides too. They're big and organized, and if you all want to play with them, you can't play their game. You have to make them play ours. Henry, White, Redding, I'm sorry but you'll be warming my bench while these fireballs try to leg this out."

Orlando Redding's deep foghorn baritone rumbled, "They get legged out alright, them big ol' white boys gone pound Carrithers in the ground."

Laughter erupted from the bench as the buzzer sounded the end of half time. "All right now, you all get in there and bring me home a touchdown." Burwell growled as the defense left the bench. The kicker was the last man off the bench and as he passed Burwell the coach caught his shoulder, "Pete I want you to kick that thing so hard they got to chase it all the way back to Indiana." The little man looked up at Burwell and smiled, "Y-yes, Coach."

The Tigers lined up at the fifteen-yard line and Pete paced back three long strides and set himself just off center from where Roundtree held the ball. When the referee blew the whistle, Pete took two long graceful strides forward and followed through with his right foot contacting the ball perfectly.

The ball rocketed deep into Notre Dame Territory. The maroon Tiger defense followed it to act as blockers for the run back. The Irish stood at the ready as the ball reached its zenith and came in deep.

Milton Carmichael, the junior running back from Davenport, Iowa lined himself up and eyed the ball as it returned to earth. He snatched the ball out of the air, impressed with the amount of steam it had, even on descent.

"Carmichael has the pigskin and is headed into Tiger territory. The Irish have fielded a bigger stronger line to run interference and protect Carmichael, but these Morehouse Tigers are like a swarm of hornets, outrunning the bigger Irish team." Avery Reed commented with genuine surprise in his voice.

On the field, Carmichael sprinted off the five, tucking the ball against his right side and hunkered low, reserving energy for a burst of speed if needed, but confident in his blockers to shepherd him to open field. He darted between two broad green backs wresting control of two maroon tigers. He slowed to change direction and felt a hand grasping at his sweater.

When the hand clenched his shoulder and he felt a second groping at his side, Carmichael planted a foot and spun down and away to the left, causing the tackle to trip. As the man fell behind him Carmichael cut right and ran full bore down the open field.

"The ball carrier leaves Irish field and is headed deep into Tiger land. He's across the fifty, the forty, and the thirty..." Avery called, sounding hopeful.

Shooting past the kicker, Carmichael thought he was home free when he heard a sound akin to hoof beats behind him. The sound of multiple pairs of cleated boots closed in despite his effort to push harder.

"And Carmichael is stopped at the twelve by Carrithers and Roundtree." Reed reported with an air of disappointment.

Carmichael pushed up and the two laughing tackles rolled away. As he gained his feet he growled, "It's not funny."

Carrithers and Roundtree clasped hands and pulled them apart and both of them laughed again saying, "Yes it is."

The referee spotted the ball as the teams moved into position. Reese and Hull were the first to arrive, stopping ten yards shy to huddle, Reese scanning the sidelines for a signal from Layton. There was none.

As the team huddled Reese weighed his options and decided on the passing option. He quickly decided to attempt to pass on first and second down and run as a last resort. "They're playing their fastest guys. We have to keep the game to our cadence. I'll lob it to the first open man, but remember these boys are fast so when you get the ball, don't stand around."

The Irish lined up, Hull in front of the ball, and Reese called the play immediately. Hull snapped the ball. Reese caught it and danced backward three steps. He counted one, two, three open receivers.

The Maroon Tigers were barely set and the faster cadence put most of their line out of rhythm. The line began to falter the moment the ball was snapped.

Reese fired the ball to Hale.

Downfield a Morehouse guard names Johnson watched the ball leave Reese's hand and shoot through the narrow opening in the coverage toward a short, stout looking lineman. The man's arms appeared unnaturally short as he reached for the ball, flexing thick fingers, the ball still twenty yards distant but closing quickly.

Johnson sprinted to intercept the ball. His heart pounded in his ears as his cleated boots pounded the earth. Hands outstretched he leapt to where the ball had been just a hundredth of a second before.

Hale snatched the ball out of the air as the red sweater flashed in front of him. He wheeled and ran for the end zone. He wasn't built for speed, but had horsepower to spare.

Johnson recovered and followed Jones and Meriwether after the loping green sweater of Hale. The three ran down Hale like a pack of hungry hellhounds. Jones grabbed for his shoulders, Meriwether for his waist.

Hale ran for all he was worth, but he just wasn't fast. He felt the weight as strong hands closed on his shoulders. He stiffened but kept running. A moment later arms clasped around his waist, and despite the instant drag he pushed onward, not slowing.

Johnson couldn't believe his eyes. The big man moved forward with two men trying to tie him up. With a burst of speed Johnson started to overtake Hale and lowered his head, launching himself, grabbing the bigger man's legs. But it was too late.

Hale tripped and fell beneath the weight of two men, his legs tied up by the third. He fell across the line.

"Touchdown, the Irish lead the Maroon Tigers by fourteen. The powerhouse Hale brought down one stride too late, maybe the Tigers should have sent a couple of extra guys." Reed sounded very critical.

●●●

On the Morehouse Fifteen the Irish toe the line and wait while the Tigers huddle. "I sense some trepidation as both team physicians minister to the line judge who stepped into the path of the Old Hardheaded, Jack Hull on the last drive. Hull picked up twenty yards and a new down. The doctors are trying to pick up what's left of the official. A brutal fourth period opening in Atlanta with the Notre Dame Fighting Irish taking on the Morehouse Tigers in an exhibition scrimmage to inaugurate or perhaps initiate the Tigers into the American College Football Association..." Avery Reed reported. His tone was as somber as the mood on the field.

Jack Hull stood off to the side of the physicians attending the fallen line judge. He was shaken and explained over and over to coaches Layton and Burwell that the man had deliberately stepped out in front of him.

Layton looked at Burwell, "What do you make of that. Sounds like somebody trying to meddle in the game."

Burwell looked him in the eye, "Looks to me like he'll look before he crosses the street next time." Layton got the message that if anyone was meddling, Burwell wasn't in on it.

The physicians hoisted the line judge to his feet and walked him off the field. For the next series of plays the referee gave Jack Hull a wide berth.

As time ran down Morehouse scored a touchdown in the final minute. The final score was 28-14. As the teams passed each other on the way to the locker rooms some shook hands, some did not. The crowds filed away and the custodians made their way into the stands to clean up.

●●●

There was little jubilation in the Maroon Tigers locker room. They'd lost to a white team from a big university on their home turf. The big city papers and radio coverage had predicted their loss. The national sports coverage had treated the game as a novelty. Only the local sports reporter from the Atlanta Beacon, Stephen Q. 'Squirrel' Jones sought to interview the coaches after the game. No radio outlet, not even Avery Reed who had provided play by play coverage for NBC radio sought post game commentary.

Squirrel Jones watched from the press box as the last of the spectators left the stands. He looked at Avery Reed who was smoking a briar pipe and packing up equipment to return to the WAGR station. "Well, here to the first of many. I guess." Jones said in passing as he turned to the sound of footsteps on the back stairs that led up to the roof where a film crew with two cameras had filmed the game for the ACAA.

"I wouldn't get used to it," Avery said, chomping on the pipe stem. He lowered the RCA 77dx microphone into the equipment case and snapped the cover in place. He exited as the first camera operator made the turn on the landing and descended the last three stairs into the press box.

"Is there any way I could get a copy of that film?" Jones asked.

"What do you want it for?" The cinematographer asked.

"I'm Stephen Jones. I cover sports for the Atlanta Beacon. All the big papers and radio treated this game like a joke. I think we're looking at the future here."

The second camera operator entered and the first one deferred to him. "There's the man you want to talk to."

After a brief explanation, the fellow nodded and said, "We make two prints. One for our archive, another for news other interested parties. You're the only one who spoke up for this one thus far. Give me your address and I'll send you the print once we're done with it."

Squirrel nodded and scribbled an address on a slip of paper from his notepad. "About how long will that be, do you think?"

The fellow smiled, "In a hurry?"

"People have a tendency to forget the punch line if they don't hear a joke a couple of times," the other cameraman interjected.

Squirrel shot him a look. "I have a column in the Wednesday and Sunday editions. And I also have daily coverage. I know tomorrow is out of the question, but I'd like to do it this week."

"I send the film to Chicago to be developed it takes about a week. I think there's a processor in Ohio, but I don't know if it would be any faster." The second man said.

"What about Brownie?" The first one offered, "Brownie's makes the medium and large format cameras and they do fast process developing for the newspapers. I think they've got a shop in Charleston, South Carolina."

"Our next job is in Charleston," The second one said in passing as he folded the tripod.

"So when can I get the film?" Squirrel asked.

"We have to film the Gamecocks season opener Friday, but it's a much bigger deal, we have to be over there by Monday to start setting up on Tuesday."

"How will I...?" Squirrel sounded apprehensive, he checked his watch. "Crap, I gotta catch Coach Layton before him and his boys get on the bus." He patted his pocked and then picked up his notebook off the desk.

The nearer cameraman called to Squirrel as he left. "Don't worry about it. I'll make sure you get it. As fast as I can."

•••

Wednesday morning Emmett Layton awoke with the same headache he'd had during the bus ride home from Atlanta. The headache had persisted the day long on Sunday. The headache and heartache associated with having his team show their rear end on the road and having taken an interview with a reporter while still emotionally charged from said rear end showing.

He got ready more slowly than normal and drove himself to the university. The small lot near the main doors of the athletic department was full so Layton drove around the side of the building and parked just outside the staff entrance. He wasn't more than ten feet from the car when he realized that the people milling outside the main entrance were reporters. Layton went to the staff door and found it locked.

With resolve he turned toward the parking lot and walked toward the front of the building. He brushed past the first two and waded into the crowd of twenty. "Coach Layton! Coach. Mr. Layton. Coach?" a cacophony of voices vied for is attention. He kept moving forward and the gang of reporters moved with him.

"Was there any difference playing a black school in the south?" an unseen reporter shouted.

"How did you prepare to face a coach like Harvey Burwell?" The reporter backpedaling in front of him asked.

"How will you stop much faster players from now on?" Another unseen reporter asked, sounding accusatory.

"Avery Reed's coverage of the game made it sound as if the Irish didn't take the Morehouse team seriously. What is to become of the Notre Dame program if you don't treat every opponent with respect?" This was question was asked by a razor edged female voice.

Layton pulled up short and looked around him. He located the sole feminine face in the crowd of reporters and looked her up and down. She wore the uniform of the Women's Army Corps.

"And you are?" He asked her, noting that she didn't look away when he made eye contact.

"Sergeant Miriam Ward, Stars and Stripes."

"Well Miriam, I can tell you that all the players and I as the coach take our responsibility as the premiere football program, very seriously. This was an exhibition scrimmage to welcome the Morehouse Maroon Tigers to a new level of play in the ACAA. Had this been an official game it would have been approached a bit differently."

Ward grimaced at him and reached into the leather satchel slung across her shoulder. She pulled out a folded newspaper, opened it so that the front page showed above the fold and handed it over. "Well Emmett, it looks as if you'll get your chance."

"ACAA bookends official season with Irish/Maroon Tiger closer," Layton read aloud, dumbfounded. "Where'd you get this? When was this decided?"

"It's been all over the radio, the big papers ran it yesterday. The South Bend Gazette is running the article from the Atlanta Beacon that prompted the decision today. It was written by some local kid in Atlanta." Another anonymous reported offered.

It all came back to Layton. He remembered answering a few questions for the kid, in a huff on the way to the bus. He hadn't been particularly polite and the kid didn't seem the least bit phased by it.

He folded the paper and tucked it under his arm. "I'll hold a press conference at noon and answer as many of your questions as I can. I have work to get done." He strode off in the direction of the front on the building.

Layton heard the telephone ringing before he got to his office. He heard the secretary answer and the moment she set the receiver on the cradle it started ringing again. This went on for as long as it took him to walk the length of the central corridor. When he entered the office the secretary, Mrs. Engle, shot him a look. She pointed to a stenographer's notebook in which she had written fifteen messages just that morning.

He was about to say something to her about the press conference when the phone started to ring. Layton picked it up, "Notre Dame Athletics, Coach Layton speaking."

There was a pause on the other end as if the caller hadn't expected for the head coach to answer his own phone, "Coach, this is Robert Fox with the Boston Globe..."

"Mr. Fox, I'll be holding a press conference at one this afternoon." Layton said flatly, cutting the man off.

"One o'clock? I'm in Boston. I can't get out to South Bend by one." The exasperated voice erupted from the receiver.

"Sir there's about fifty reporters from the other papers outside. I'm sure if you call any one of them they'll tell you that I'm not talking until then." Layton explained. The frustrated fellow hung up.

Layton exhaled sharply as he lowered the handset to its cradle, "How long has this been going on?"

"It was ringing when I got here at seven-thirty." Mrs. Engle said with a tacit smile.

Layton rubbed his chin thoughtfully, "I suppose now would be a good time to kiss and make up with the radio station and have this press conference there so it goes out to all these people and settles that phone down so we can get something done."

Mrs. Engle smiled for real this time, "I'll call them right away."

On October 1, 1938 when the Irish played Kansas State for their first official game the papers were still talking about the exhibition with Morehouse. It was as if the entire schedule was to be ignored and the nation was looking forward to the Irish returning to Atlanta eleven weeks hence.

•••

In Atlanta, Coach Harvey T. Burwell coached his team to keep their eyes on the ball in front of them and not the ball ahead of them. The publicity had been good for Morehouse, the colored sports programs, and the Negro colleges. However, it had been bad for the focus of the players. He had known it would be, but it was an easily equated trade.

On September 27, 1938, Coach Burwell's morning was first interrupted by a telephone call from The Chicago Tribune. The secretary was out of the office and Burwell picked up the phone on the third ring, "Morehouse Athletics, Coach Burwell."

"Coach Burwell this Mike Kulczyk, with the Chicago Tribune. Your Maroon Tigers have certainly caused quite the stir with their initiation into the ACAA." The husky ethnic voice growled.

"We didn't make our best showing that day. I expect a whole lot more out of my players." Burwell clipped.

"Oh, from what I'd read in the coverage provided by the Atlanta Beacon's Stephen Q. Jones, it sounded like a pretty tight contest." Kulczyk offered.

"How long has this been going on?"

"Pardon me. I thought you were going to ask me for a rebuttal to Avery Reed's radio broadcast." Burwell apologized.

"No I hadn't heard. Something I've learned about covering sports in the radio age, its always done on the announcer's day off, and it's the guy on the boss's list who has to cover it."

Burwell digested this, but didn't reply on the subject. "So what can I do for you Mr. Kulczyk?"

●●●

The season drew on and became long for Coach Layton. As his team played a fine season to little fanfare with the constant focus of the public on the looming season closer with the Morehouse Maroon Tigers standing shadowed in the doorway like an angry father, there to punish him one last time before he could put it all to bed.

It brought him pride and satisfaction to watch his players weekly. The efficiency of Hull and Reese, the steady strength of McGinn, but the winning had become so regular that it was almost pedestrian. He knew it was past time for a younger man to take over.

Monday morning following his Week 7 post game remarks with Tim Hill, and the now ubiquitous gaggle of reporters Layton retreated to his office to prepare for his final two games as head coach of the Notre Dame Fighting Irish. He felt completely used up, as if he lacked any further inspiration to carry on.

He pulled out a desk drawer and there laying atop a conspicuous brown composition book was an aged bottle of Park & Tillford Rye Whiskey. He set the bottle on the desk and reached into the drawer for a small crystal glass.

He didn't immediately find the glass and lifted the brown notebook out and laid it on the desk. He bent over the drawer and rifled through its contents. The glass was on the bottom, very dusty, and slightly stained with the residue of spirits.

Layton uncorked the bottle and poured the little glass full. He gulped the dark amber liquid and shuddered. He filled and drank three more times and was raising the bottle for a fifth belt when there was a knock at the door. Before He could respond or hide the bottle, Mrs. Engle opened the door. When she saw the bottle and the glass, she exhaled sharply in exasperation.

Mrs. Engle stepped in and pushed the door closed behind her, "Emmett, what are you doing? There is a man here from the Atlanta Beacon to speak with you."

"Tell him I'm not seeing any reporters today." Layton ordered.

"You tell him. He's been in the book for a week. I've been the secretary here for a long time and I have never been asked to cover for the coach while he sat at his desk and got drunk." The old gal's feathers were ruffled and Layton's ears began to ring.

"Okay." He ran a hand over his face and stepped into the small lavatory to splash water on his face.

Mrs. Engle was still standing near the desk when he came out. Her disdain was plain and unquestionable. "You might want to put that bottle away. I'm certain that Mr. McGhee and the athletic board would take a very dim view of your drinking on the job."

Layton almost felt bad, but only momentarily. He realized that her tight wrapping had annoyed him for a long time. The rye whiskey had finally loosened his tongue enough to say whatever he thought. "Right across that field," he pointed to the east, across the practice field, "Right over there. Hell, not a mile from here, a bunch of guys in brown frocks drink on the job every day." He corked the bottle and downed the glass of whiskey he'd poured previously. He returned both to their berth in the desk drawer. "Now, if you'll kindly show in Mr. Jones."

"Mr. Layton, one of us isn't going to survive this season." Mrs. Engle started.

"I'm done with it as soon as we get back from Atlanta. I told them I was done before we started. It hasn't been the same since…" Layton trailed off, feeling suddenly very drunk and quite sick.

"I'm going to put Mr. Jones up in a hotel and you can see him tomorrow. You are going to go home, lie down and sleep this off. You might be finished, but this university is not. I will not allow you to drag our boys down with you." Mrs. Engle said sternly. Layton didn't argue and laid his head on the desk.

A little while later Layton became aware that someone had again entered his office. He swiveled his head up and rested his chin on the desk. Mrs. Engle was there, as well as George McGhee. Layton closed his eyes again and laid his head on the desk again.

"Emmett!" McGhee growled to no avail. "Get the door, I'll take him home." Layton felt himself hoisted to his feet, and felt powerless to resist.

●●●

Sometime in the night Layton's whiskey soaked mind began to dream. He remembered the biggest game of his career as a player. The memory of that season flooded back to him and he remembered. He was younger then, he played with seniors who'd known Gipp.

He dreamed of Knute Rockne pacing in the locker room lecturing the current team, and that thunderous and confident voice. "In the backfield, I want Hull, you and McGinn, Rice, and Nevius. Always the success of any team is based on teamwork, gentlemen. Don't forget, men, you gotta get 'em on the run, you gotta go, go, go! Don't stop until you're over that goal line! Today is the day we're gonna win. They can't beat us, dead simple, that's how it is. You guys are the first team men; go in there and fight, fight, fight!"

Layton sat bolt upright, suddenly awake, Knute Rockne's classic parting shot still ringing in his ears, "What do you say, gentlemen!"

When he arrived at the athletic complex, Mrs. Engle was out. He gathered his messages and walked into his office. There on the desk lay the brown composition book he'd placed there the day before. Today he recognized it immediately.

He dropped the message slips on the desk and picked up the composition book. His fingers caressed it almost lovingly as they traced over the wonderful imperfections of the well worn cover. He opened it and read, 'Playbook, Notre Dame Football. Presented to Emmett Layton by Coach Knute Rockne.'

Suddenly inspired he grabbed a black canvas binder off a cluttered shelf and sat down. His program and playbook was more complex and contrived than the little brown comp book, but he felt that he and therefore his program lacked some passion of the bygone era. He opened both books and got to work.

●●●

The Week 9 game against Wilberforce closed the season on a sour note, with a 24-3 loss, the only blemish on an otherwise perfect regular season. Coach Harvey Burwell indulged the recent interest in him and his team by the newspapers and radio by being candid on the subject of the team's performance and respectfully diplomatic on the subject of the looming season closer with Notre Dame, which would be a full regulation game.

The following morning he stepped into the pulpit at Holloway Baptist Church to deliver the gospel message of thanksgiving that he always delivered on the last Sunday of November. A number of players were among the regular congregation, which was not unusual. There was one white face among the sea of black ones. Burwell smiled inwardly to see Stephen Q. Jones in church.

After the service as the congregation filed out, Burwell stood near the door shaking hands and greeting each man and woman as they left. Stephen Jones was the last man in line and Burwell squeezed his hand a shook it.

"Good to see you Coach," Jones said with a smile.

"Good to see you, likewise Mr. Jones." Burwell said warmly. "How was your trip up north?"

Jones sighed deeply in spite of himself. "I don't know how much I ought to say." He said thoughtfully.

"That tells me a lot. You didn't go all that way for nothing, Did you?" Burwell asked with a note of concern in his voice.

"Well it was supposed to be a one day up and back, but I got the feelin' something was going on. When I got there, well Layton was in his office, but the secretary went in and didn't come out. When she did come out she was in a complete fluster, rushed me off to the hotel, and fast."

"Hum, that don't sound right. I hope everything was okay." Burwell said quietly.

"When I saw him the next day, he was intent on his work. The secretary was out and the office door was open. I found him doing his homework. He was distracted while I was interviewing him, like he had a whole lot on his mind. I heard a couple of the prep team talking during practice..." Jones trailed off.

Burwell raised an eyebrow. He wanted to ask, but wasn't one to encourage gossip. Jones was watching him as if he was waiting to be asked.

Just then Mavis Burwell entered from the parking lot, "Are you ready Reverend Coach?"

Burwell grimaced at her, "Can't you see I'm having a conversation?"

"Invite him to Sunday dinner and you can jaw to your hearts content while I'm getting the meal together." Mavis said as she turned around and headed back to the parking lot.

Burwell smiled and turned to Jones, "Do you like chicken fried steak?"

●●●

It seemed to Coach Layton that every newsstand at every stop on the bus ride from South Bend, Indiana to Atlanta, Georgia carried at least three of the big papers with blanket coverage of the looming game between the Irish and the Maroon Tigers. There was also plenty of repeat coverage from the smaller papers, largely just syndication of the big paper coverage. Then there were the smaller papers like the Atlanta Beacon, and writers like Stephen Q. Jones.

Layton had bought himself as much ill will as any coach could afford, and yet the fellow didn't seem to be bothered in the least by it. He conducted the interview professionally and went back to Atlanta, where he wrote a balanced profile of each coach. The Opinion, Editorial, and Op-Ed columnists on the other hand, were brutal. The only consolation there was that the further south he traveled the opinion seemed to slant back in his favor.

In Clarksville, Tennessee, they stopped for the night at a motel of moderate size. The man at the counter recognized him and wanted to talk about his strategy for beating the undefeated Morehouse team. Layton did his best to excuse himself from the conversation. In the end, the man just wanted to wish him well. Layton just wanted to get it over with.

In Virginia, Layton encountered well wishers. In North Carolina and South Carolina it was a more tepid reception from younger people and more encouraging from older people. He was shocked to hear a shriveled old shrew with rotten breath hiss at him from the counter of the restaurant, "Be sure and whoop that uppity bunch of...," the door closed behind him as he left, not in the mood to dignify the woman's remark with a reply.

Thursday afternoon when the bus arrived in Atlanta the reception was much different and more hospitable than it had been weeks earlier when they'd come for the exhibition scrimmage. Once the team was assigned rooms and settled, Layton went to his own room and locked the door. He didn't open drapes or turn on the radio. He laid back on the bed, kicked off his shoes, and slept.

Friday brought an early morning run, and a brief impromptu practice on the Carver High School athletic field. After running calisthenics drills for twenty minutes, the offense and defense squared off for a first team scrimmage. The second team likewise played a crunch time game, running only special plays designed as practice tools. Reese and Hull worked on changes to the snap drills with Peter Brady the likely heir to the starting quarterback position.

•••

In the tunnels, at opposite ends of the stadium the teams were lined up to run onto the field. A late autumn drizzle pattered outside. People in the stands sought to shelter themselves with umbrellas, newspapers, or programs. The voice of Avery Reed blaring from the loudspeakers seemed to make the afternoon breeze all the colder.

Coach Burwell stood in the wing of the tunnel opening watching the rain. He glanced at his watch just as the buzzer signaled 12:30pm. He nodded to Carrithers to take the team onto the field. The man nodded and cinched the chinstrap on his leather helmet as he roared and ran out of the tunnel, followed by the rest of the Maroon Tigers.

The applause from the crowd was less than enthusiastic as the rain redoubled its efforts. Coach Layton gave Hull the nod and the big man raised a fist and ran onto the field like a Viking Berserker. The rest of the Irish were with him as he went to center field for the coin toss.

Avery Reed sounded astonished a moment later when he reported the official's hand signal. "Jack Hull team captain for the Irish calls it, and they Irish elect to kick?"

O'Rourke lined up and on the whistle, he sent the ball deep into Tiger territory. Roundtree pulled it in at the fifteen and was off like a shot running back from where it came.

"Roundtree's got it and he's out beyond the twenty... The Thirty!" Reed announced.

●●●

Roundtree tucked the ball in close to his side and his legs uncoiled like steel springs under tension. He shot between Hull and McGinn and made the twenty and thirty yard lines before the blockers had a bead on him. When Carmichael came for him Roundtree rolled right to avoid his outstretched hands and then juked left to slip a tackle. He sprinted toward the end zone but O'Rourke hit him head on and both men went down.

"Roundtree is stopped at the Notre Dame twenty five by the kicker, O'Rourke." Avery Reed announced.

On the Notre Dame sideline, Coach Layton gave the rally sign. The team knew the drill and the defense headed for the line of scrimmage. The few members of the kickoff package who were part of the offense double timed off the field toward the bench.

"Quarterback Roosevelt King has led the Maroon tigers through a perfect season thus far. This final game, not popular with proponents of the status quo, but the ACAA and college sports have other ideas." Reed digressed.

On the field Roosevelt King lined up behind the center. A hush fell over the crowd as Clevin Mayes gripped the ball. He listened to the hard count and intuitively knew King's hands were open behind him. Mayes glanced into the intent eyes of the man in front of him and snapped the ball.

As if in slow motion King watched the ball as it left Mayes hand and came toward his hands at a sharp upward angle. He took the ball from the air, rolled left and came about. King found his open man. He fired the ball as the giant, Hull drew a bead on him.

Hull pulled off and watched the ball's downfield track. The Morehouse player caught the ball on the run. He gained another five yards before his progress was halted by Irish tackle Dolph Schmidt.

As the line shifted Layton called out from the sideline, "Hull!" The big man cocked his head, nodded in recognition and ran over to the sideline.

"Yes Coach?"

"Remember the Phalanx we practiced this week?" Layton demanded.

Hull nodded his affirmation.

"Lock it up." Layton ordered.

Hull nodded and headed down field. He ran past the Morehouse huddle and gave the rally sign to the Irish. As the team gathered he said, "Twins back, Phalanx Defense, man on man." The team didn't speak, but to a man they grunted or nodded their understanding.

•••

In the Morehouse huddle King encouraged his team and waited for a play call from the bench that didn't come. He preferred a fundamental game, so a pass after the runback was conventional. A completion with gain was good news and his assumption that the Notre Dame team would expect a run was correct.

King looked down field and saw the Irish break their huddle. He didn't recognize the formation the meandering players were moving into. He turned back to the huddle. "Mayes, you read this one. Something is different over there. If you can set up for a lateral to Carrithers, if not on the snap send it back and we'll bootleg."

"The Maroon Tigers struck deep on the first play and threaten from the Irish twenty." Avery Reed announced as the Tigers took the line.

King didn't like the look of the Irish Defense. The look was like something out of a military manual instead of a football playbook. He didn't want to admit it, but they looked like a bigger and more intimidating team. For a moment he second guessed what he'd instructed the team to do and remembered Coach Burwell's words, "Morehouse wins by playing our own game, and making other teams play our game. They might be bigger and stronger, but they don't know our game. Make a decision and stand with conviction."

On the snap, King rolled left and Mayes fell back three steps. King gave the ball a lateral pitch to Mayes who hooked back and ran downfield toward the line of scrimmage. As he crossed, the blockers shifted and he was taken down at the nineteen.

●●●

On the Morehouse sideline Coach Burwell watched as the bootleg play collapsed. He wanted to shake his head. He had tried to train King not to play simple box to box football with seasoned teams. "Clutch," he growled at a husky dark skinned man hunched forward on the bench behind him.

The young man stood up, "Yes, Coach?"

"Get in there, relieve Mayes. Tell King to run flat rock skip." Burwell growled.

Clutch double timed it to the line of scrimmage and conferred with King who called to Mayes, "All right Mayes, Clutch is in for this series."

Mayes frowned at the second stringer and shouldered past him. Clutch who wasn't tall lined up across from Hull, casting a shadow every bit as broad. He listened as King counted it off and snapped the ball.

King had it and rolled right looking for an open man. The blockers engaged and the tackles and ends fought to get down field. Clutch tied up Hull and drove him back nearly a yard. King caught sight of one and then two defenders breaking through.

As the defenders encroached, King tucked the ball and ran through the opening created by Clutch as he continued to drive Hull backward. King sidestepped and threw off a tackle. Rocking to the right in an attempt to dodge a blocker he ran into another stout green sweater and before he knew what had happened the ball was stripped away.

●●●

"Notre Dame Sophomore Bart Graham goes into assist McGinn for the tackle on Tiger's Quarterback Roosevelt King and comes away with the ball. He's back across the line of scrimmage." Avery Reed called out, excitement in his voice.

On the field Graham shot past the line of scrimmage and saw open field ahead. He ran headlong for the goal in the distance. His legs pumped and his heart thundered in his ears. The roar of the crowd in front of him and the booing crowd behind invigorated and energized him.

"Graham is across mid-field. It's a foot race here in Atlanta as Carrithers tries to leg out Graham who has a significant lead." Reed announced.

Graham had no idea he was being pursued. He poured all his energy into his legs and ran for all he was worth.

"Graham at the thirty, the twenty, the ten. Touchdown, Notre Dame is the first on the board here in Atlanta."

The entire Notre Dame Defense poured into the end zone and congratulated Graham. They retreated toward the sideline as the Offense hit the field. Across the field, Coach Burwell was giving last minute instructions to the return team as they headed for their positions.

"O'Rourke sends it uptown. Not a great kick by comparison, Carrithers has it at the thirty." Reed reported.

Carrithers watched the brown laces rotate as the ball descended. He started forward, checking his lane and caught it on the run. His avenue started to close and he darted left, heading across the forty-five searching for an open lane. Two steps ahead he saw Mayes cut off a blocker. Carrithers juked to the left and cut around Mayes.

In his escape minded myopia, Carrithers neglected to look before he leaped and tripped over a tangle of bodies. Fighting to maintain footing, Carrithers spread his arms trying to steady himself. Along with the clownish elongated stride, he looked like an angry goose attacking a rival. Eventually momentum got the better of him and he went down.

Many spectators noticed and laughter erupted. Avery Reed commented, "After a reasonable advance, Carrithers goose dance brought the runback to a humorous finish."

The Irish Defense gathered. The Maroon Tiger Offense took the line. The Official who spotted the ball blew the whistle. King stood up trying to read the Defense. He called the play and Mayes snapped the ball.

As King backpedaled, the receiver Ashe slipped his block and shot down field. King sent the ball away as Hull knocked him off his feet. The mis-thrown pass wobbled in the air, just out of reach on its downfield arc. Ashe reached for the ball, but tipped it.

McGinn watched as the wobbling ball came down. He ran toward the receiver. He almost smiled as the tipped ball caromed up and over a falling body. Just as he was launching himself to tackle, Ashe grabbed the ball and fell on it. McGinn landed on him and from there the pile ensued. The referee and both side judges ran on to the field, blowing their whistles.

"Ashe and the pigskin are down, under that pile someplace. A quick pause while the officials sort this one out. Its heating up here in Atlanta as the Notre Dame Fighting Irish have come to reckon with the undefeated Morehouse Maroon Tigers. WAGR and NBC Radio will return after this announcement from our sponsor." Avery Reed announced as a murmur spread through the crowd.

The referee and the side judges meticulously peeled the players off the pile. The first four came off with little incident. The further down the more entwined the men were. At the bottom of the pile, they found Ashe clutching the ball with both hands and McGinn also trying to pull it in.

The officials stood there looking at the way the two were situated for so long that it drew the attention and focus of both coaches. Layton made his way over and arrived just before Burwell. They regarded each other momentarily and Burwell spoke first, "I'm glad I don't have to sort this out and explain to somebody why their guy din't come up with it."

Layton smiled in spite of himself and nodded his agreement. "Ain't gonna be pretty, no matter how that comes out."

Both of them looked at their respective teams, and then Burwell went to stand by Layton. "If it comes down to a coin toss I'm okay with it." Burwell offered. "Thanks. McGinn will want to plead his case, but I think your man fell on it first." Layton said quietly.

Finally, the Referee pulled McGinn's elbow and told him to get up. McGinn pushed himself up and rose to his feet looking expectantly at the officials. Moments later, after a brief conference, when the referee pointed to the Morehouse end zone, McGinn's temper exploded and he released a cloud of profanity and squared up to Burwell.

Layton got between the two, "McGinn haul it in. You're done for the day. I warned you about your conduct the last time we were here."

"Looks like McGinn is finished for the day and Russell will finish the afternoon at Pulling Guard. And that will do it for the first quarter." Reed announced, sounding bored as the buzzer sounded.

•••

At the bottom of the pile, they found Ashe and McGinn ...

"We've gone from a late autumn drizzle to an outright downpour here in Atlanta. When this one's over they may call it The Water Bowl." Avery Reed announced over the din of the downpour, which sent many spectators scrambling for cover.

Hull planted his feet and felt the suction of the mud as he crouched. He set his weight forward, intent on driving through the man in front of him. A rivulet of sweat and rainwater ran down the muddy face in front of him and Hull almost smiled.

King called the play and Mayes snapped the ball. Hull surged forward and made contact. Mayes was unable to get traction and was easily moved despite his resistance. Hull pushed past him with little trouble and assaulted the quarterback.

King saw him coming and scanned the field for an open man. Hull hit him head on, driving him back and planting him in the mud. King started to sit up, but his sweater held him down, he had to roll onto his side and peel the heavy woolen fabric out of the muck. It was wet, heavy, and cold.

"The Maroon Tigers lose three and its third down. They may call this one early if this rain persists." Reed mumbled, as if he were eating.

King and Hull sneered at each other as Avery Reed's words sank in. King growled, "No way!" Hull offered him a hand.

The referee spotted the ball on the Morehouse 37. The Morehouse offense lined up behind the ball. Their feet sloshed in an inch of standing water. Plumes of muddy water swirl around the booted feet.

Mayes gripped the ball and pressed his thumb into the laces. He gave a look up and down the line and waited for the play call. When it came he was caught off guard. Hull was driving him back before he realized that the ball was slipping away. Somewhere in his mind he knew he had blown it and had to try to get it back. To him this was the most important play of his career. It was his last game.

In his feverish retreat from Hull's relentless plowing, Mayes tried an about face, and slipped. Hull, sensing his reduced balance pressed forward. As Mayes fell he held the ball out, extending his arms.

From somewhere, Carrithers ran by at speed, snatching the ball out of Mayes hands. He tucked it close and ran for all he was worth. He turned the corner like a speed skater and ran down field. He weaved through Russell and Carmichael, who ran headlong into each other in their sloppy haste to arrest his advance.

Sure he was free Carrithers slowed and it proved to be his undoing.

"What is Carrithers doing?" Reed announced, exasperated.

The second guard, Rousseau, a lanky high school track and field star, ran down Carrithers, and dragged him to the ground at the two yard line. Carrithers gathered himself as Coach Burwell called time out.

Burwell, who was usually calm and understanding with his players, lost his temper. "Carrithers! What is the name of John Brown are you doing? Are you trying to give up this game? Get on that bench." He jabbed a thumb over his shoulder, and whirled toward the players already on the bench. "Clutch, you're in for Mayes." He turned back to the gathered team. Mayes, you're staying in, but you're playing at running back."

Mayes watched as Carrithers stalked toward the bench. He glared at Burwell, "He thought he was home free."

Burwell seethed, "You don't ever quit until you are home. The only thing almost gets you in this life is the opportunity to be the first loser. Now get out there before I fill your spot."

"Looks like Carrithers has been sent back to school. Clutch in for Mayes and it looks like the Center Mayes will fill in at running back. Good thing its short, Burwell's replaced a jackrabbit with two snappin' turtles." Reed reported to the shrinking crowd.

The teams moved into position at the line of scrimmage and Clutch glared at Hull. King Counted it off and to no one's surprise, Clutch gathered the ball and plowed into Hull full bore. Hull dug in to halt the shorter man's advance.

Clutch, who trained pushing and pulling a loaded hay wagon, also dug in. He slipped Hull's attempt to seize his shoulders, feeling the big mans fingers clawing for purchase. He slipped his shoulder left as if he was going to juke, and Hull almost went for it.

Hull tried to grip Clutch's shoulders. Suddenly the stout center tried to dart around him, causing Hull's grip to fail.

Clutch felt Hull release him. Instead of slipping by and allowing himself to be tackled, Clutch lowered his shoulder and fiercely drove Hull backward.

Surprised, Hull pumped his feet, trying to get traction, or leverage against Clutch to no avail. No matter how he fought to stop the man's progress he failed.

Clutch was still driving at Hull when he heard the referee's whistle. He stopped and looked around realizing he was in the end zone and the referee was holding up both arms, indicating a touchdown. A moment later the buzzer sounded.

"And that does it for the first half. The Morehouse tigers lead the Notre

Dame Fighting Irish by six in Atlanta. Please join us for the second half of this very wet season finale after these announcements from NBC Radio." Reed announced the halftime break and then segued into the weekly news.

•••

In stark contrast to their earlier run out from the tunnel both teams returned from half time at a low tempo trudge. The rain had slacked to a constant drizzle, but a cold breeze was picking up. The men were cold and wet and the break had done nothing to mitigate their weary chill.

The Notre Dame offense took the field with Carmichael as the return man. He liked to line up deep and run out to meet the ball. It was his style to catch it on the run. He scanned the opposite end of the field for the kicker.

Downfield Pete picked up his feet several times trying to get a sense of the footing. He approached the ball and paced off three long strides directly behind the ball. He turned quickly and on the sound of the whistle he took two powerful strides. When he planted his left foot to follow through with the kick, he started to slide off balance.

Carmichael watched as Pete stepped into the kick and slipped. He could feel the man's pain as the booted kick took off on a low, wobbling, end over end trajectory. He knew it would never cross the fifty yard line. He ran for it, covering the sucking muck as quickly as possible, but doubtful of arriving before the ball was out of play.

Pete cursed himself the moment his right boot plowed through the mud and scooped under the ball. He knew it was a bad kick, but there was no way to take it back. He ran after it, leading the defense. The best he could hope for was recovering the ball before the Irish returned it for a touchdown.

In the press box Avery Reed was on his feet, "I don't believe it. Carmichael actually has a hold of that dead duck and he is taking it home."

Despite the bad kick, the ball had more juice than Carmichael had anticipated. He pulled it out of the air on its downward arc at the forty. He ran another fifteen yards before being tackled at the twenty yard line.

•••

The clock read 1:30 remaining in the third quarter. The referee spotted the ball and Reese and the offense took the field. The last thing Layton said to Reese before he left the sideline was, "Keep it short and simple."

Hull snapped the wet ball. Reese made the grab and pivoted on his heel, scanning for an open receiver. There was no one open short and the only man who reliably knew what to do with a lateral was holding the line. He scanned left and right and was considering an end run when a maroon sweater slipped and fell on his face, creating an opening in the line.

Suddenly Russell was loose and running down field. When he was clear and started to turn Reese fired the ball. The pass rocketed toward Russell.

"A basket catch and Russell is on his way." Avery Reed sang.

Russell stumbled into the end zone with three Maroon Tigers hot on his tail. He fell to his knees and slid a couple of feet in the cold mud. He held the ball out in front of him and just looked at it. The cheers from the diminished crowd made him smile. He slowly got to his feet and handed the ball to the referee.

"That will do it for the third quarter. Irish even it up, eighteen all here in Atlanta." Reed reported with little reaction from the remaining crowd.

When the buzzer sounded the end of the third quarter the somber mood on the field was one of relief. The men were cold and wet. The rain sapped strength and will. The cadence of the game had slowed to a crawl. The stands were nearly empty save for the hardiest of boosters, fans, and family.

It was with resignation that the offense and defense exchanged for their counterparts. Roundtree ran O'Rourke's kick back to the fifty before being tackled by Russell and Carmichael. Layton sensed the grim tone and called timeout.

●●●

Layton had no remarks in mind as his team slogged toward the sideline. As the men gathered he remembered a similar time when it was he who wore the wet, mud caked green sweater and the man on the sideline was a far better man in his estimation. When the last man arrived, he channeled Knute Rockne and gave the last and best motivational speech of his career. "Men, none of you knew Knute Rockne. But you all know of the great legacy that he left us at Notre Dame. I had the pleasure and privilege of playing for and assisting him. He was the best player, and coach, and leader I've ever known. Let's win this one, this last one for me and many of you, for Knute." His reverent tone and intensity concentrated as he glared at each one to a man. "Hull get out there, lead these men. Let's do what we came here for. Reese, get the ball to every open man. If there is no open man, run it in yourself for a score. You linemen are capable of more than being logs that must be climbed over, you can run and you can catch the ball.

Guards and tackles, remind these men of who we are and what we do. Out there is a battlefield and your enemy today are men of worthy character. They've played a good and honest game with a lot of heart. But we are Notre Dame. We are champions. Now get out there and win this last one."

When the timeout was called, Coach Burwell ran out and met his team on the field, beckoning the entire team, including men from the bench. "Gather round! Gather round I say! We're right down to it. This is the last period of football many of you will ever play. To us this is just another game. For us this game is supposed to be a big deal. To them this game is just another dog and pony show because they are the big time. No matter what happens time will go on, but you need to consider what this game means to everyone else, the people who are not on this field today. What we do here. The character we show, the heart with which we play, will be a mean by which black men in uniform and black mothers in Mobile will be measured for years to come. For some of you this is the last game of organized ball you will ever play. Make it a memory worth having, because you are going to hold onto it for a long time. Be men of honor, of strength, of character. We didn't invite them to Atlanta, to our house, to show us how they play football. We brought them down home to teach them how we play football. Go teach these Fighting Irishmen how Maroon Tigers play this game."

Neither team seemed particularly boosted by their coach's efforts. The rain continued to fall as the men lined up. Mayes snapped the ball to King, who threw a short pass to Ashe for a loss of one yard. The second down play, a cross route run was stopped short of the line of scrimmage for another lost yard.

"Third down, King's got it. It'll be a Hail Mary. Roundtree's not going to get it. The ball made the trip for nothing." Reed growled.

Roundtree carried the ball back to the line of scrimmage and handed it over to the referee. "Well, at least one of you didn't run down there for nothin'." The official said kindly. Roundtree shot him a look, "We're down here cold and wet, he's up there having a beer and telling people what football looks like." The referee squeezed the water from the sleeve of his sweater. "You don't say."

Layton watched the blighted spirits of the players on both teams. He recognized the effects and hoped that his team could dig deep enough to pull together and score. When the Morehouse Quarterback threw the dud pass he anticipated that Burwell would call for the punt. When the Morehouse offense headed for the sideline he called his team in and fielded only players who were fleet of foot. Carmichael was the return man, but he sent every Irish player who could bring the ball down field in a hurry onto the field.

"Morehouse will punt the ball away. It looks like Layton has decided to bring the first team in and let the bench have a go at the Tigers." Reed's bored and disinterested commentary echoed through the mostly empty stadium.

Pete stepped into it, the ball went high, and long. It returned to earth, caught by the hands of a Sophomore Running Back named Paul Cruse. Aside from apparent surprise at receiving the ball on the first play of the first regular season game in which he'd actually taken the field, Cruse reacted perfectly.

Cruse picked up a lane of travel behind two other receivers from the prep team who were having their first outing. The pair defended the initial wave of blockers and eventually neutralized ten yards down the field. But Cruse ran on.

As he crossed the thirty the coverage was heavier. He avoided a tangle of green and red sweaters by cutting across toward the Morehouse side belt. As tackles encroached, Cruse got so far outside that Coach Burwell considered the direction he would go to avoid being trampled.

At the last second before crossing the sideline and going out of bounds Cruse made a sharp cut and poured on the speed. He weaved his way through the last of the coverage and glanced left and right. He turned his head and looked forward, just in time to slam into a Maroon colored wall named Clutch. The last thing Cruse remembered before the lights went out was the ball coming loose.

Clutch ran right through Cruse who didn't fall fast enough. He scooped the ball up from its end over bounce and chugged into the fray.

"I don't believe this. The Irish Running Back was running the return route. Perfect, textbook coverage blocking. He cut outside to deliver the mail to the Morehouse bench. He was headed home when he piled keister over handlebars into Clutch and the ball came loose. Clutch got it on the bounce and is taking it back to the equipment locker." Reed suddenly realized he was at a sporting event.

Clutch's heavier frame didn't avoid coverage, he plowed through it. He wasn't as fleet of foot as Cruse and made a more direct route. He was cold and wet and tired and every waterlogged, mud caked step was an agonizing irritation. He was ready to log this one and call it a day. But it wasn't over so he pounded onward.

Clutch crossed the thirty yard line with four green sweaters closing in. He was running for all he was worth but it just wasn't enough. He felt arms close around his waist and the weight of the man slowed him down. As he fought for traction in the mud, he was sandwiched between two more tackles and brought down at the nineteen.

Even before the referee whistled the play dead, Coach Layton was on the field trying to change the ruling and have the ball brought back to the place where teammates were hauling Cruse out of the mud. "You're bringing that back right?"

The referee spotted the ball and turned to walk toward the side belt when Layton cut him off. "Hey, Ref! I'm talking to you." The man paused and looked up at him. "You're taking that back right?" He gestured to where Cruse was still out on his feet, supported by two teammates.

"Coach it was a fair call. The runner contacted the blocker and dropped the ball. The blocker caught it on the first bounce and returned it." The referee stepped around him and Layton grabbed for him, but Hull and Reese were there.

"What in the hell has got into you?" Hull demanded. Layton blew him off and walked to the bench and sat down.

"He's decided he's done." Reese said as he walked away. Hull started to follow him off the field, but was directed to go in at Middle Linebacker and send the second team guy to replace Cruse.

On the snap King fired a short pass to Mayes who advanced the ball four yards before being tackled at the fifteen. King glanced at the clock as the teams moved and lined up. He shook his head.

Clutch snapped the ball and King rolled back and turned. He pumped and stopped short. He watched as the line started to collapse as if in slow motion. In a sea of rising green and shrinking maroon, he saw Roundtree through a narrow opening in the coverage. Roundtree turned and as he did so, caught the unexpected ball and was almost immediately tackled on the nine yard line.

"New set of downs for the Maroon Tigers as the clock stops with one minute left to play." Reed announced.

King recognized the Irish defense formation that had caught them earlier. This time they didn't look like a bigger more intimidating team. To him both teams now looked the same, wrung out. He tried to remember what play he'd called before, and why it was unsuccessful.

●●●

As soon as the ball was in motion the Irish Phalanx closed to a man. The two tackles fell back deep. Hull got the slip on Clutch and powered past him to attack the quarterback. Hull launched himself at King, but realized the quarterback didn't have the ball. Sliding and the rolling to his feet Hull looked downfield.

Somehow, on the snap, the Morehouse Center had made the drop and King and the ball carrier had exchanged places. Hull started downfield, but the runner had been stopped at the three yard line.

"Second Down and short, thirty seconds remain on the game clock here in Atlanta. This one will go down as the Mud Bowl." Reed groused.

●●●

King called the play and Clutch tucked the ball. He surged forward and clashed violently with Hull. He held the ball tightly and tried to power through. Hull's footing began to fail and Clutch was pushing through when the defense collapsed and brought him flailing to the ground on the one yard line.

"Third Down, on the one." The Referee called to the line judge.

On the count Clutch faked the snap and rolled back. He shot a short, quick lateral pass to Mayes. Mayes ran just behind the line of scrimmage toward the Irish sideline. He handed off the ball to Roundtree, who cut sharply and launched himself toward the end zone.

Two mud-caked Fighting Irishmen seized Roundtree and halted his movement just eighteen inches from the end zone.

King called a huddle and as the team gathered he gestured to the clock. "This is it. No matter what happens when we line up, we either tie or we win. Don't let there be any question, get in and get open. Clutch, Mayes, read it and make your call. We'll all be waiting. Clutch you call it off, Mayes you clear your throat real loud if you see something that changes the call."

The Irish were aligned along the line of scrimmage. Mayes was the last Maroon Tiger to take his position. Clutch waited, listening for Mayes, who made no sound. On the Whistle he counted it off.

He tucked the ball in and faked the lateral to Mayes. The defense locked in and stopped forward motion of any runner or receiver, save for one. Clutch lowered his shoulder and battered Hull on a three step running start. The Old Hardhead was rattled and knocked clear, opening a hole in the defense that immediately began to close. As Clutch broke across the line of scrimmage the Irish phalanx closed around him threatening to halt his motion. Then Clutch got mad.

With the Irish defense closing around him. With one man tearing at the ball, another at his waist, and a third pulling on his sweater, Clutch roared and drove forward. He pulled the three off their balance and he managed four strong strides. As the buzzer sounded the end of the game, Clutch stood knee deep in a pile of football players so dirty and caked with mud that it was near impossible to distinguish one team from the other.

They were all finally equal as Avery Reed made his final remark, "Unbelievable here in Atlanta. The Morehouse Maroon Tigers have beaten the Notre Dame Fighting Irish twenty-four to eighteen in an inch by inch battle for one hundred wet, muddy yards of real estate. This has been Avery Reed for WAGR and NBC-Radio."

As the players from both teams shook hands and shared greetings and congratulations, Coach Burwell and Coach Layton met on the fifty yard line. They shared brief remarks and Burwell offered a hand. Layton looked at it for a long moment before shaking. A moment later each man nodded to the other and walked off in the direction of his locker room.

In the coming days newspapers across the country ran first coverage and syndicated articles on both teams written by Stephen Q. Jones. The post game interview with Harvey T. Burwell was very modest on his part, crediting the win to the players and only crediting himself with minimal guidance. When asked about Coach Layton he said only that the man seemed troubled.

Coach Emmett Layton refused interview requests and promptly resigned on his return to South Bend, Indiana. His home was quietly sold to a local merchant and Layton left town. He was never seen publicly again. Rumor had it that he retired to a family farm in Mussel Shoals, Alabama.

The End

4th & Inches Essay

I love the craft of telling a good story. I try to breathe real life into the characters and their surroundings. I try to put seemingly ordinary characters, some as humble as can be, in extraordinary circumstances. I don't like to compare my work to that of other writers. It is a comparison of apples and oranges. To say one author's story isn't as good, or is better than another's is a matter of opinion and perspective. For an author to indulge in such is an act of vanity alone.

I'm both self published, and published traditionally in a variety of media-news, blogs, magazine, short stories, novellas, and novels. Fiction and non. The worst thing any author can do, and especially those who have achieved success is to discourage the efforts of others. While no one's success is guaranteed, we must all help each other the best we can.

Fourth and Inches, as the name implies is a story about struggle. I think deep within most people there is a turmoil or conflict that drives us to do our best. I've also realized during the writing process exactly how little I actually know and understand about the game of college football. For rulebook purists who will have their personal copies of The NCAA handbook for Collegiate Football 1935 on the desk as they read this tale, I'm sorry but you will find it lacking... If you're there for the real story, the people story, then you could find few more interesting characters than the late Burwell Harvey.

I took on this project without a clear vision in mind. I knew I wanted to do a golden age college football story. The details of that and its difficulty for me personally might have been a deal breaker had I not happened upon Coach Harvey completely by accident whilst searching for something else. Harvey was the very definition of homegrown talent. He was a student who played and coached, then became a professor and coached, and innovator of more than just football, though he had a very credible record off 11 titles in 15 years.

Coach Layton, of course represents most assistant head coaches who have been brought up in a program in the shadow of a public hero... He's an unknown who knows the drill and is left to continue the legacy of someone else, who may or may not have truly been the hero personally that the public held in such high esteem.

I found the writing of this story incredibly challenging. Football was a completely different game than we see today. The rules were more literal and less open to interpretation. I couldn't find any films with audio from that era, and only one radio broadcast that I could actually follow.

In the end I did my best to cover an old fashioned football game in the style of a Monday Night Football game. The radio announcer plays a key part in bringing you the story and I thought a more journalistic style might be more appropriate for a story where there is a continuously shifting point of view. I hope you enjoy 4th & Inches.

•••

J. WALT LAYNE - lives in Springfield, Ohio. He is a veteran of the US Army, a married father of three, and a voracious reader. A prolific writer, he is the author of Frank Testimony a legal thriller set in Bedford, Mississippi in the 1950s. He is also the author and creator of The Champion City Series of pulp detective stories to be published exclusively by Pro Se Press (March 2013). He has written a laundry list of articles for Backwoodsman Magazine and is the former Op-Ed columnist for The Albany Journal (Albany, Georgia). You can catch up with him on Facebook as Author J Walt Layne.

HILLBILLY LIGHTNING

By

John Rose

There it was! Right in front of Bill Youngstone who hadn't really believed it existed, but seeing is believing! It was a well worn building alright, that much Bill had been told. It definitely needed a paint job as it was difficult to tell what color it had originally been. Most likely, it had been a light brown or tan color that was now blending into the weathered gray of old wood. It was a two story building with lots of windows on the second floor, but it looked to Bill like they had all been boarded up from the inside.

About where the second floor would have begun, there was a weather beaten sign that had the name of the place. And if you didn't look carefully, you would not have even noticed it.

The sign read: *Captain Comet's Combat Club.* All in what had at one time been bold dark letters. Now they were barely decipherable.

Bill Youngstone had been trying to locate the legendary Club for a lengthy amount of time and now that he had actually located it, he had a depressive feeling about wanting to cross the street and knock on the door. The place looked dark and the young man did not believe anyone was actually there.

The building had two plate glass windows, one on each side of the recessed doorway. Placed in front of the window on the right was a wooden bench that appeared to have been there as long as the building itself.

The young man looked down at his dusty high topped shoes and saw the laces dangling there with sand burs sticking to them. He frowned. The bench would be a good place to sit down and pick them out, if nothing else. Bill shifted his duffle from his right hand to his left,

He knocked lightly on the door and waited. After a moment or so, he rapped again, somewhat louder. As he waited, he tried to peer through the dark dust and cobweb covered glass of the front door, but the slight bit of light he thought he could see far back in the building looked more like it might be a reflection of something.

Bill was sitting on the bench, the leg of his overalls pulled up as he used the blade of his jackknife to scrap the burs from his frayed shoe laces, his duffle bag sat at his feet.

He was lost in thought and did not realize a wagon had pulled to a stop in front of him until he heard the voice.

"Hey, kid," the man called, "you lookin' for a job?"

Bill's head popped up. "Well, yeah, I could sure use one. What kind of work are you doin'?" he asked.

"Farmin'," came the reply. "About six miles north o' here. If you want to work, climb in." the fellow said.

Bill quickly closed his jackknife and returned it to his pocket. As he rose to get in the wagon with the older fellow, he dropped his duffle in the wagon bed near the front.

"Where you from?" the farmer asked.

"Southern Missouri, the Ozarks," replied Bill.

"Oh, hillbilly from Arkansas, huh?"

"No, just the southern part of Missouri. Down around the Lake of the Ozarks, place called Hollister."

The farmer grunted and was silent. Bill felt like the fellow had already made up his mind that he was from Arkansas and not Missouri.

"What is your name?" he tentatively asked the farmer.

"Charles," the man replied. "Charles Weatherbe. And you are?"

"I'm Bill Youngstone." the young man replied.

"What brings you to this part of the country?"

"Lookin' for work, I guess," Bill replied.

"You guess? You mean you don't know?" the farmer replied in a rather disgusted tone of voice. The driver turned and gave the boy a hard look.

Just then an automobile came around the corner and headed directly toward them. Old Charles took a firmer grip on his reins, but his team ignored the noisy contraption that rumbled past them.

"Ain't quite got used to them things!" the farmer growled.

"You ain't got an automobile?" the boy asked.

"Yeah, I got one," came the reply. "My two boys drive it mostly. I still prefer the team. Gives a man time to think. Today they needed some exercise, so I'm drivin' 'em."

They were silent for a short bit and then Bill decided to try again.

"I come out here lookin' for work," the young man began. "Thought maybe I could get on with a harvest crew or something. But it doesn't seem like many folks are hirin' much. Back in Pratt they told me about a fellow out here that had a club where he hired young men to help him win money at county fairs and special occasions. Stuff like that. Thought maybe I'd give it a try. I was told, if I was real athletic, he'd probably take me on."

The farmer remained silent, but did nod now and then.

"I don't know exactly what this Captain does, but I've been told I'm kind of athletic. Just thought it might be somethin' I could do. Do you know anything about the Captain or his club?" Bill asked.

"Nope," the farmer replied. "Around here, everybody kind of minds their own business."

They rode in silence for a while. Then Bill spoke again.

"Do you know this Captain? Ever see him around?"

"Yeah, I've seen him. Looks about like everybody else. I don't rightly know if he does county fairs and things. Fact is I don't know what he does."

"When do you suppose would be the best time to catch him at his club?" Bill asked.

"You figurin' on runnin' out on me?" the farmer asked, giving his passenger a glare.

"Oh, no," Bill responded quickly. "I just thought your job wouldn't last forever and when I was through, I might try this Captain fellow again. That is, if I could ever find him."

Farmer Weatherbe nodded.

"You know," Bill began again, "I been in three different towns lookin' for this guy. Then I find his club right in Highland! I had begun to think those fellows giving me information was just pullin' my leg."

"Just where else did you look for this Captain fellow?"

"I was told he had an office in Sawmill. But it seems like nobody down there had ever heard of him. Then I was told he might be the fellow in Clearwater. That didn't pan out either. Then a fellow swore up and down he had an office located in Buckboard. Claimed he was his uncle or somethin' like that. Then I come to Highland and there is a building with a big sign sayin' it was *Captain Comet's Combat Club*. Don't that just beat all?"

"Sounds like you was gettin' the run around alright," chuckled the farmer.

Again, they rode in silence for a while.

"What kind of work are you going to have me doin'?" Bill asked after another mile had passed.

"Oh, the normal kind of farm work," the fellow replied. "I've got a big garden patch and there is always work that needs to be done in there."

"Any cleaning of barns or stables?" Bill asked.

"Yeah, there is that," nodded the farmer. "We haul a lot of that muck out and spread it on the garden where we work it into the soil. Good fertilizer. Makes for a good crop."

Bill nodded his head silently. Maybe, he thought, he could stick it out for a day or two, get a good meal and maybe be on his way. This wasn't sounding like something he really wanted to do.

Charles turned the team off the main road and onto a driveway that led a good quarter of a mile up to the farm house. The driveway ended in a loop with a double garage located in the middle of the circle. Parked in the garage were a late model automobile and a half ton pickup. The farmhouse was located on the upper side of the slope on the right hand side, while the barn and corrals were located on the left and much farther down the slope

The farmer pulled the horses to a stop in front of the yard gate. "Up there," he said, pointing up the hill and beyond the house "is where the garden is. It's on the back slope of the hill. You can see the windmill right there on the top of the hill and there is a stock tank full of water which I use for the garden. Do you reckon you could go up there and turn the spigot on the tank to start the water running down a row of tomatoes? Tomatoes take a lot of water, if you're going to get a good crop."

"Yeah, I can do that," Bill grinned.

"Alright," said Charles. "I'll take the team down to the barn and get them taken care of and then I'll be up to show you what I need done in the garden patch."

Bill hopped down from the wagon seat and lifted out his duffle. The boy carried his belongings up the hill and dropped the bag near the windmill, while the farmer took the team on to the barn.

●●●

Charles parked the wagon in the shade of the barn, unhitched the horses and led them through the building. While inside, he removed the harness and hung it up. Next he released the team to drink from the horse tank and graze in the pasture.

Then Charles Weatherbe proceeded to unload several sacks of feed he had picked up in Highland. Once that was finished, he picked up a grocery sack from the wagon and headed toward the house. He looked up the hill but could see nothing of the young man he had hired.

Bill Youngstone had gone directly to the tank. He found the spigot fastened in the bottom of the water tank and tried to turn it. Bill was not very familiar with pipes and water faucets and when he could not get the lever to turn on the water, he backed up and planted a heavy kick with the sole of his shoe against the spigot. He broke it and the water gushed out.

He thought it looked like it was running out pretty fast but he did remember the farmer had said it took a lot of water to raise tomatoes. So that was probably about right.

Looking around, Bill saw a cherry tree that was laden with ripe fruit. Pulling out his pocket knife, he walked over and cut off a branch about three feet long and just covered with red ripe cherries.

He found a shady spot under a black walnut tree and sat down to enjoy the fruit. Bill ate fast and it wasn't long before he had the branch stripped clean of the juicy fruit. He sighed and lay back against the trunk of the tree.

"What the blazes have you done!" came a loud bellow and Bill Youngstone leaped to his feet to face a very angry farmer.

"How in the world did you tear that faucet off the water tank! And what the dickens are you doing cutting branches off my cherry tree?"

The farmer's face was red and his eyes were shooting sparks. He grabbed the bare cherry branch from Bill's hand and began to rain down blows across the hillbilly's back.

Bill gave a loud squawk at the first stinging stroke, grabbed his duffle and broke into a run for the driveway. The farmer was howling mad and was right behind the young fellow continuing to strike him across the shoulders as they ran.

The farmer's wife heard the angry yells and the howls of pain and when she ran to the screen door, she saw her husband and the new fellow racing by at full speed. They rounded the house, went down the cobblestone walk and through the yard gate. The young fellow was now pulling away from her husband and running down the driveway as though he were being chased by a wild Indian.

Soon Charles came back by the house, hurrying toward the water tank to get the water stopped. It was very clear that he was highly irate and the wife decided she would just stay clear of the man for a while.

●●●

It was six miles back to Highland and Bill was so wound up he didn't actually walk for several miles, although he did slow down to a steady jog once he had outdistanced the farmer.

The young fellow did not know what he would do once he was back in town, although he assumed he would find a barn or someplace where no one would see him and he would hole up for a while. This was not unusual for him as he had basically hitchhiked and walked all the way from southern Missouri westward. When it came nighttime, he just slipped into some place where he was somewhat protected and went to sleep.

At times he would find a garden or someplace where he could pilfer a bit of food and that kept him going. If he could have just found that fellow, Captain Comet, surely everything would have worked out.

Bill was a tow headed young man somewhere between sixteen and eighteen years of age. He was fairly tall and had a broad set of shoulders. He had passed out of the eighth grade and had spent some time in high school but just felt like school was not for him. He had actually been enrolled in high school three different times and when he had quit for the third time, the principal had told him he would not be allowed to enroll again. That, if he wanted a high school education, he would have to find another school.

Although more boys were now getting a high school education than in years previously, there were a great many that did not go beyond the grade school years. Most dropped out to go to work and help support their family and times were hard all over the country. Work was not that easy to come by and many jobs were not that well paying.

It was dusk when young Bill entered town and walked down the main street. He was tired and hungry. Without thinking, he was walking toward the weather beaten building that had the sign saying it was *Captain Comet's Combat Club*. He came to a stop and looked at the dilapidated place.

Carefully he approached the front door again. And once more, as he looked through darkened door, it appeared that he was seeing a small light in the back of the building. There wouldn't be any sunlight shining in at this time of evening.

Bill moved down the narrow space between two buildings, eventually coming out at the backside of the Captain's Club. There were a number of evergreen trees growing there and quite a bit of Spirea bushes along the sides of the backyard, interspersed with Lilac bushes. All in all, the backside of the building was blocked off from view very well.

As he moved silently along, he could smell food and his stomach began to growl. After all, it was supper time and food would be cooking in a variety of homes.

The young man walked all the way to the alley and moved over directly behind the Club building. There was a woven wire fence there and he gently opened the back gate and walked into the yard which was well covered with growing bushes.

He approached the back door. There were two cement steps leading up to a small back porch. Bill figured two guys could probably stand on the porch, but a third would make it very crowded.

When he looked in the back door window, his heart skipped a beat as he again saw a small light! Someone was here!

Bill took a deep breath and knocked.

It seemed to take a long time, but the door was finally opened and a young man stood looking at him.

The hillbilly stood silent, looking at the fellow at the door.

"Well, what do you want? You're the fellow who knocked," the young man finally said.

"Oh, uh, is this the place of Captain Comet?" he asked in a raspy whisper.

"Who wants to know?" the man asked, realizing he had a very nervous young fellow standing before him.

"I'm Bill Youngstone, from Missouri," the boy replied. "I came to see Captain Comet."

"Wait right here and I will check," said the young man, turning away from the doorway.

In a few moments, a middle aged man with receding hairline came to the door. He appeared to have been well muscled out at one time, but now seemed to have more flab than muscle. He had a bib around his neck as if he had been eating.

"What can I do for you?" the man asked.

"Are you Captain Comet?"

"I've been called that," the fellow replied.

"I'm Bill Youngstone. Came from Missouri. I heard you sometimes hire on young men with athletic ability and I'm lookin' for a job."

"Huh, Missouri, eh," he said as he stuck a toothpick in his mouth. "How'd you get out here? Got some relation or sumthin'?"

"No, I just hitchhiked. Mostly, I walked."

"You must want this job awfully bad, to walk all the way from Missouri to get it."

"Well, I'm tired of goin' to school and my folks been telling me for as long as I can remember that I'm too lazy to every amount to anything. I think they are wrong, though, and I want to prove it."

"What are you good at?" the older man asked.

"Uh, what do you mean?" Bill asked. "I can do a lot of things, most of 'em not real well."

"Well, you said you had some athletic ability," the man replied. "I just wondered what you were good at."

"Oh, I'm a pretty good runner. Ain't many people can catch me. I can go distance real good," Bill grinned.

"When did you eat last?" the man asked.

"About an hour ago," Bill said. "I had a few cherries."

"Naw, I meant, when did you have your last meal?"

"Oh, well, I haven't exactly had a meal in several days now, but I get by."

"How about if you come in and eat with us and we'll kind of talk about what you can do and then see if you really have an interest in joining our group. I kind of have a feeling you may have been misled about us. But, we'll see. Come on in."

Bill stepped inside the doorway and dropped his dusty bag off to one side, out of the way.

The man turned and led the way back through the hall a short distance and then they turned through a pantry that had shelves lined with jars of canned food. The man opened another door and they emerged into a lighted room where a table was set and there were three fellows seated and eating. Bill noticed the windows were all covered.

"Boys," said Captain Comet, "this is Bill Youngstone and he would like to join our organization. He looks a mite hungry to me, so I thought we'd feed him and see if he still thinks he wants to work with us."

"Sal, bring out another plate," the man called toward and open door that must have been a kitchen.

"Now, these men are Sam, Mark and Larry," he said indicated each fellow as he said the name. Each one nodded in return.

"This new guy is Bill, from Missouri."

Bill raised his hand in greeting and then a young woman was entering the room with another plate heaped up with steaming food. Bill's mouth started to water immediately.

"Have a seat right there," said the Captain. "This is Sal, my daughter, and she helps us out by preparing meals when we are going to be here to eat."

"Howdy, ma'am," mumbled Bill as he sat down.

The girl placed the full plate in front of the boy and laid down a set of silverware for eating.

"Thank you, ma'am," the boy said softly.

"I am not 'ma'am,' I am Sal," the girl said. But she smiled at Bill when she informed him.

It had been a while since young Bill had sat down to a full meal and he quietly made the best of this one, although he was aware of the men around the table watching him. When he would glance up, he would see them grinning at him. He knew he was coming across as a very hungry person.

"Would you like seconds?" asked Sal.

Bill nodded.

"I'll just bring you another plate," the girl said. "There is pie for dessert," she added as she returned to the kitchen.

By the time the meal was over, Bill was well fed. In fact, he was stuffed to the point where he almost felt bloated.

The others had all finished a bit ahead of him, but they had had a head start. Now they were just quietly waiting.

"Feeling better, Bill?" asked the man at the head of the table.

"Yes, I do and I sure thank you," the boy replied.

"Alright, let's get down to business," the man said. "First off, I am Matt Fenwick. That worn out sign was up there a long time before I bought this place. Had I known I was going to get stuck with that name, I'd have taken it down... maybe."

Bill nodded. The other three young men were all leaned back in their chairs and everyone of them had a toothpick sticking out of his mouth.

"You say you think you have some athletic ability," said Fenwick. "What makes you say that?"

"I spent a little time in high school," the boy replied sheepishly. "I tried to make sure I went in the spring when they had a track season. I liked to run and I could beat most everybody. Coach said I was pretty good and he wanted me out for the other sports, but I was just too busy."

"Busy doing what?" asked Fenwick, although he knew the answer he would get.

"Workin'," Bill replied. "Trying to help out the family. Times are hard, ya know."

"You say you liked school when you were out for track?"

"Not exactly," replied the boy. "I liked track. Liked to run. Didn't much care for the school work but that came with the track. So I went."

"You liked distance, huh?" mused Matt. "That is not what a lazy fellow does," he added. "Lazy fellows are lookin' for a short sprint or the broad jump. Ever play football?"

Bill, who had been looking down as they talked, suddenly looked up and grinned. "Yeah, I liked football but my folks wouldn't let me play. Said I might get hurt and they couldn't afford no doctor bill!"

"Did you like carrying the ball?" Matt Fenwick asked.

"Oh, yeah, sure! I liked carrying the ball and I got good hands for catching passes. Liked to tackle, too! Would have liked to have played more, but, you know, parents got the last say."

"Where did you run your long races?"

"When I was in school, the mile was the longest race and I always ran it, even when I was a freshman, 'cause I could beat everyone else."

"You ran some races that were not school runs?"

"Yeah, whenever I could find one. Usually there was one around fair time. And then sometimes when a couple of parishes would get together for a Sunday picnic, there would be a long race, just to pass the time, you know. I ran those whenever I could find them. Sometimes there was something on the Fourth of July."

"Win 'em all?" asked Fenwick.

"No, I didn't win them all," he replied, realizing he may have been set up. "There were times I just didn't run well or there was some older guy who was just flat out better than me. I won my share, though."

The room was quiet for a full moment as it appeared Matt and his crew were all in the process of thinking.

"Bill," the man finally said, "have you ever done any boxing?"

"Oh, no," the boy replied. "My folks would have never let me do something like that!"

"Was there any boxing or boxing clubs in your area?" asked the man.

"I don't think so," Bill replied. "Never heard of 'em, if there were," he added. "I think there were probably some boxers up at Springfield, though. Don't know for sure."

"And you never checked it out, before walking all the way out here?"

"Actually, I came out here thinkin' I could get a job in the harvest fields," the boy replied. "It was after I couldn't get a job, that I started thinkin' about runnin' again. There was a fellow in Pratt that suggested I look up this Captain Comet. He couldn't tell me much about him, though."

"You know you can't make a living running, don't you?" asked Sam, from the other side of the table.

Bill nodded mutely.

"Tell you what," said Matt Fenwick. "You get a good night's sleep and we'll go back out to the farm tomorrow and see you do some running."

"Farm?" questioned Bill, thinking of Charles Weatherby. "What farm?"

"My brother-in-law owns a farm a few miles out of town to the west of here," said Matt. "My boys all work out there. Sort of helps pay for their keep. Plus we can take time off whenever we need extra time for something.

"Did you like carrying the ball?"

Seth, my sister's husband used to do some boxing, so he understands what it is we are trying to do."

Bill nodded again.

"Sal," called the man to his daughter, "we're going upstairs. You can clean up in here when ever you want."

"Okay, Dad," came the reply.

Matt Fenwick led the way to a flight of stairs leading up over the pantry where they had entered the room. Bill thought again how odd it was that no window was uncovered in the dining room. Upon reaching the top of the stairs, the man punched a button and the lights came on.

Bill was the last in the line of people ascending the stairs and when he reached the top, he stopped in awe. The room was large and spacious and seemed like it must cover the entire second floor of the building. Again, all the windows were covered.

What the boy was staring at was a gymnasium for training. There was a large tarpaulin spread out in the middle of the floor with large black lines painted on it forming a square. When Bill stepped on it, he could tell there was a layer of padding beneath it.

As he looked around he saw an area where there were a number weights and benches. There were also several punching bags hanging down from the ceiling. There were enough jumping ropes hanging from a hook for a dozen athletes to be jumping rope at the same time. The boy was impressed.

Along the walls on one side were several bunks. Bill was sure this was where they would sleep. With that thought in mind, he wondered just how odorous the place would be after a bunch of fellows had worked out. Later he found out about the fans and the vents.

The following morning, after a light breakfast, Matt Fenwick brought around a small pickup which he parked in the back alley. Sam, Mark, Larry and Bill all climbed into the back while Sal got into the front with her dad.

Matt let the clutch out and they moved down the alley toward the street and the edge of town. They were soon on a sandy road.

"There is Mollie," called Matt as they turned into the driveway of the farm.

A young girl, perhaps twelve years of age, was riding toward them on a brown and white paint pony. She grinned and waved and then picked up her lariat and began twirling it as though she were going to throw a loop on the pickup.

Everyone was laughing. Sal was waving from her window. The fellows in the back of the truck stood up to see what was going on and about that time, the paint decided there was enough commotion and slid to a stiff legged stop.

Young Mollie came tumbling out over the top of the pony's head, frightening it even more than it already was. The horse began bucking and kicking and the lariat was tangled around the young girl.

Suddenly, eyes rolling wildly, the pony broke into a dead run coming right by the bed of the pickup. Mollie was bouncing along in his wake screaming frantically.

Without thinking, Bill stepped up on the side board of the pickup bed and leaped, grabbing the running pony around the neck. He gripped the animal solidly and let his weight pull the head down to the point where the animal finally went over and landed on the ground.

Matt Fenwick had slammed the pickup to a stop and was out running toward his floundering niece.

The horse was kicking and expelling snorting grunts of fright as he struggled.

Matt lifted the terrified girl and quickly had her extracted from the binding rope.

"Okay, Bill! You can let him up! But hang onto his head!" the man yelled.

The boy let the horse get straightened around and his feet under him. Then he surged to a standing position, snorting and blowing. His eyes were still rolling in fright. Bill kept an arm around the animal's neck and talked continuously to the frightened beast. Gradually the horse calmed down.

"My God, Bill," exclaimed Matt, "I think you may have saved Mollie's life! Those rear hooves were mighty close to her head!"

After taking the spill from the horse and bouncing along the ground, Mollie appeared to be okay. However, she hung frantically to her uncle and cried. Her mother and father were both running toward the scene.

The mother, Matt's sister, was also streaming tears and she quickly grabbed her daughter holding her carefully, but also tightly.

"I think she is alright," said Matt, "but I expect we should take her into town and let Doctor Browne check her over. Might be something we can't see that should be attended to, you know."

"I'll get the car," said Seth. "Fern and I will get Mollie in to the doctor and it shouldn't take too long. We'll be back out here afore dinner," he said as he turned to run toward a garage where his automobile was parked.

Fern had Mollie standing on her own feet and then she looked toward the four boys standing off to one side. A tall blond haired boy was holding the bridle of the obviously distraught pony.

Matt saw his sister looking at the fellows and came over to her. "That tall one is Bill," he said. "He is new with us and he is the one who leaped out and stopped that runaway. He may have very well saved Mollie's life or kept her from a serious injury."

"Actually," said Fern, "I saw it from my kitchen window. I heard your pickup and I just looked out to see if it was you and the boys coming. So I saw the whole thing. I think Seth did, too, because when I ran out of the house he was already running from the corrals."

"Oh, I was so scared!" breathed Mollie, in a very shaky voice.

"And rightfully so, honey," said her uncle. "That was something to go through!"

When Seth brought the car up, he let Fern and Matt get his daughter settled into the back seat while he came over to shake hands with the young man who had rescued his Mollie.

"I can't thank you enough," he said. "I want to visit with you more when we get back from the doctor's office. In the meantime, Matt can tell you what to do with that horse."

"Fine. Thank you, Sir," Bill replied softly.

Seth Harkins, his wife and daughter were soon on their way to see the doctor over in Center View since there wasn't one in Highland.

●●●

The boys walked Patches back to the barn while Matt followed along behind with the pickup and Sal.

When they parked, Sal got out and went to the house to see what Fern might have had going that needed attending to. The girl was still somewhat shaken at what she had witnessed.

"I think we just need to leave Patches tethered to the manger in his stall," said Matt. "He'll be fine there and Seth can take care of him when he comes back later. If, for some reason, they are not back by noon, we'd probably ought to give him some water, though."

Matt and the boys went out to the back corral and worked on a fence until it was almost dinner time. Seth and the girls weren't back yet, and Sal wasn't sure what had been planned for the midday meal. She was waiting until her aunt got back before starting anything major in the lines of cooking.

"Not a problem, guys," grinned Matt. "We'll just do a workout on an empty stomach, then rest a bit and then eat. We'll be fine."

Matt led them to the barn loft where there was much in the way of equipment and the fellows went to work. Sam and Mark donned gloves and began working on punching the bags and using footwork as they moved. Larry began jumping rope and Bill decided to lift some weights. They worked for a while and then rotated positions. Finally Larry and Bill laced on gloves and began punching.

When everyone was warmed up and the sweat was running freely, Matt brought the training to a stop.

"It is my understanding," he said, as the fellows stood panting and wiping sweat from their brows, "that Bill has never had anything to do with the sport of boxing. Is that right, Bill?"

"Yes, Sir, that is correct," the boy replied.

"Then how do you account for your footwork, son? It looks pretty good and I dare say I've never seen a green boxer that looked any better. Are you sure you've never boxed?"

"Positive," said Bill softly. "I'd really rather run, but..."

"We might find something for you along those lines," said Matt, "but I wouldn't hold my breath, were I you. However, I'm standing here watching you move and you're no plodder! I'm impressed. And the quick thinking you did getting that horse stopped, didn't hurt anything!"

Bill just grinned.

"Speaking of that horse," said Matt, "maybe you ought to take him out to the horse tank and water him. Make him drink slow. He has a tendency to want to guzzle the water as fast as he can suck it down!"

Bill went to the stairwell and down to get the horse for watering. As soon as the boxers could look at the open end of the barn loft and see Bill with Patches, Matt Fenwick spoke.

"What do you boys think about our new recruit?" Captain Comet asked.

"I think he looks pretty good," said Larry. "Needs a lot of work, but it looks like he might have what it takes. He claimed to have a reputation for being lazy, but I'm beginning to believe he is just feeding us a line. I like the kid, though."

"What do you think, Sam?" asked Matt.

"I need more time before I start trying to give an opinion," the boy said. "I'm like Larry in that I like the kid. And I don't see any laziness, either. I dunno what that is all about."

"Two things," spoke up Mark. "We need to run a couple of tests. One would be to see if he can really run the way he says he can. The other is we need to get him to box for a round or so and just see what he does. You can tell pretty quick if he's had some boxing in his past. It won't matter what he says."

"Do you like the boy?" asked Matt.

"Hadn't decided until he pulled that fool crazy stunt of jumping out of the pickup on that horse! That could have got Mollie killed! And I don't much care for show-offs!"

"I don't think Seth and Fern saw it the way you did," said Matt softly. "Take it easy around them."

"Yeah, sure Matt," the boy replied.

"Bill is bringing Patches back," said Larry. "He'll be in the barn in a minute."

"Alright boys, when Bill gets up here I want to show him some basic moves with his feet and his arms. How to protect himself. How to do a little bobbing and weaving, trying to make himself hard to hit. That ought to begin to tell us what we want to know."

"Just let me take him on," said Mark. "If he is a fighter, it'll show up right away."

"Hey," said Larry, "he is our stablemate, whether you like him or not. Who knows, he might be a real contender someday. You see those shoulders he's got on him?"

"After you show him some basics," pleaded Mark, "let me spar with him a little bit. That'll tell you everything you want to know!"

Bill appeared, coming up the steps to the hay loft. He grinned at his new friends.

"Come on over here, Bill," said Matt Fenwick. "I'd like to show you some things that you need to know to get started as a boxer."

●●●

The man spent half an hour going over stance, foot movement, positions in which to hold the arms, how to cover up to keep from absorbing so many hits. Finally he covered the four basic punches used in boxing.

"Now, Bill, there are a lot of things that are illegal to do when you are in a boxing match and we'll go over those when it comes time. Meaning, when you start to do something that will cost you the match, we'll tell you! How are you feeling?"

Bill shrugged and grinned. "Pretty good, I think."

"Fine," the man said. "Would you like to do a little light sparring with Mark for a couple of minutes?"

"I guess so," said Bill.

"Now, remember the things we just went over, because you're going to need everyone one of them plus a whole lot more if you stay in this game," said Matt.

Both boys had their mitts on and tied. Matt added a little tape to cover the laces.

"Not too hard, but try to look like boxers," the man laughed when they were ready. "Okay, go after it."

Bill did not have a boxer's skills, that was obvious from the start. But he seemed to pick up quickly on what Mark was doing. The thing he had to his advantage was his quickness. They had gone for about a minute and a half and Matt was thinking about stopping them as he had seen all he needed to see to know the boy had been telling the truth. He was a green boxer, but there was talent that could be developed.

Evidently Mark sensed it was about time for the bout to be over and he had, as yet, been unable to force Bill to show he had had previous training for boxing. He stepped in quickly and slammed a jab into the side of Bill's head that rocked him.

Bill stepped back slightly stunned. Then he heard Matt telling him to get his hands up and he realized Mark was coming after him again. Then the boy revealed what one could have called his secret.

Bill sent a jab straight to the point of Mark's chin. Bill's secret, the length of his reach, was out! If it could actually be called a secret because all one had to do was look to see the boy had long arms.

Lightning played in front of Mark's eyes and he staggered backward. Larry and Sam both leaped out to catch him before he hit the floor but they were too late. Mark set down hard, somewhat dazed with the turn of events.

"Sorry, Mark," said Bill as he bent over the downed fighter and the three fellows trying to help him.

Mark gave a painful groan and tried to get to his feet. Larry and Sam lifted him up and then steadied him as he caught his balance.

"Let's get him out to the horse tank and get some water on him," said Matt. "That'll bring him right around."

"For just sparring," grumbled Mark, "he hit pretty hard!"

"Who threw the first really hard punch, huh?" asked Sam.

"It looks like, with Bill," said Larry, "he'll play the game however you want to play it. I'd just practice with him and not really try to have another bout."

Mark nodded and grumbled something that no one understood.

The water from the horse tank brought Mark around rather quickly and Bill apologized again for knocking him down.

"That's enough," said Matt. "You don't need to apologize to someone in the fight game for setting them on their butt! It's all part of the sport!"

The Seth Harkins vehicle came rolling into the yard. The man and his wife both got out but there was no Mollie.

"They think she is okay," were the first words out of Seth's mouth as the group approached. "However, they wanted to keep her for a while for observation. We thought that was a good idea 'cause she took some real hard bounces behind that horse! Something could still show up!"

"We'll have something on the table in about forty-five minutes," smiled Fern and she gave a light wave to Bill.

"How is it going this morning?" asked Seth as the group moved toward the barn.

"We got that back fence looking pretty good now," said Matt. "Then we spent some time in the loft. "Mark and Bill went for about a round. It is our first look at the kid. Would have liked for you to have seen it. Kind of help me determine what we got here."

"Think he might be any good?"

"Could be," nodded Matt.

"Matt," called Sam, who was walking behind the two men with the other boxers. "Bill, here, wants to know when we're going to do that runnin' you was talkin' about?"

"When do you want to run?" Captain Comet asked, looking back at the boy.

"Not right after we eat," said Bill in a low voice. "It would be good to run right now, while I am somewhat warmed up, or we'd need to wait until much later in the afternoon."

Matt was grinning and nodding. "You sound like you've done some running, alright."

"How about if you guys run a race around the corral and barn here?" asked Seth.

"How far is it?" asked Bill.

"The boy likes distance," added Matt.

"This would be around five hundred yards, give or take," said Seth. "Just how far were you thinking?"

"Oh, I'd like to go a mile or two," replied Bill.

"You do like to run, don't you?" laughed Seth. "I used to do a little running. Didn't amount to much and I always felt like it was probably a benefit for my boxing training. Lot of boxers don't actually run all that well."

"I don't think these other fellows are going to want to go for a mile," said Matt.

"Especially me," said Mark. "I'm not up to that yet!"

"Oh, I thought I was running by myself," said Bill, somewhat surprised. "Back home, I could never get anybody to run with me. Finally quit trying."

"These guys need the running," said Matt. "We just aren't going to go as far as you are used to going. We do the one lap that Seth suggested."

●●●

They opened a couple of gates that would allow them unrestricted access to a loop around the corral. The start would be at one corner of the barn and they would go out around the corral, across the small back pasture and around the opposite side of the corral. They would finish on the corner of the building, just the barn width from where they started.

"Okay, boys," said Matt, "here is what we're going to do. I want to see how well Bill here can actually run, so I am going to stagger you fellows out in front of him for a ways. Bill will start right here at the corner. I'm going out twenty steps and that is where I'll put Larry. Another twenty steps and we'll have Sam and Mark another twenty steps beyond that. Mark's probably still a little dizzy, so he may need that lead."

The boys were all to watch Seth and when he dropped his arm they were to start running.

"Ready!" yelling the man and the boys crouched. "Set!"

On the set command, Mark began running. Seth dropped his arm immediately to let the other fellows go after him.

They were half way through the race when Bill caught Larry who seemed to be the best runner of the three. They ran together and soon caught Sam, who just shook his head and began slowing down. Mark was only ten strides in front and there was something like a hundred yards left to run.

Bill picked up the pace, leaving Larry behind. He caught Mark fifty yards from the corner of the barn and the runner was struggling. He kept looking over his shoulder at the oncoming Bill Youngstone.

Mark was running tight and with his fists clenched. Bill could sense the boy was agitated. He swung very wide as he passed the staggering runner. Sure enough, the guy's arm swung wide in an effort to hold Bill back, but there was no contact as Bill had swung wide enough to make sure of that.

He kept looking over his shoulder at the oncoming Bill Youngstone.

Once Bill had passed, Mark stopped and walked. Larry and Sam both passed him for second and third places respectively.

"I reckon that answers your question," murmured Seth who was aware that Matt was trying to determine just how much of what Bill was telling him could be believed. "I think the boy is a runner."

The fellows began moving around to cool down after the run and then gradually came back to the area where the two men were visiting.

"I believe I could have beaten him," said Mark, when he joined the group, "if I hadn't been hit so hard when we were just sparring!"

"Hey, you know who threw the first really hard punch," said Sam. "You tried to set him down and it backfired! Just wise-up and take your medicine! He's on your side, you know!"

"From what I see of Bill," said Larry, "he isn't any dummy! He knew you were going to swing at him when he went by and he made sure he was far enough away you couldn't hit him."

"Go to the tank and wash off," said Matt. "Then let's go up to the porch and rest a bit before it's time to go in and eat."

•••

Each day the group of four athletes would go out to the Harkins' farm where they would do some farm work, get a workout in the barn loft, and so some running on the road.

Bill was picking up the skills of boxing at a rapid rate and they often had short sparring bouts in the evenings. However, Matt did not let Mark have another shot at the new guy because he was sure it would be nothing more than a chance for the older boxer to try to even the score.

The work, however, with Larry and Sam benefited the young boxer a great deal. Footwork and upper body motion was critical for the new guy and Matt could see improvement every day. Positioning of his hands, both to cover up and to strike at his opponent was vastly improving.

•••

"Boys," said Matt, one evening, "tomorrow we are going to take a train trip to Colorado Springs. I've got some spots reserved for you at the Spring House and we'll get you lined up with some competition once we get there."

"Wow," exclaimed Larry, "I thought it was about time we were getting in some work with live meat!"

"Bill, you ever ride a train before?" asked Matt, looking at the new guy.

"You're wanting me to go, too?" asked the boy.

"You can learn a lot by just watching," nodded Matt, "but have you ever ridden on a train?"

"Yeah, I have," replied the boy. "Generally, I just hop in an empty box car when it starts to move out. Be quick and careful and nobody ever knows you're on there!"

Matt chuckled. "What I was referring to, was where you buy a ticket and ride in a coach like normal people."

"Never did it that way," smiled the boy, shaking his head.

"Bill is not gonna fight, huh?" asked Mark. "Seems kind of a waste to take him along."

"Like I said," replied Matt gently, "he can learn a lot by being there. He has already greatly improved his skills, just in the short amount of time he has been here."

"I think, if you're going to take him," said Mark, "you'd ought to put him in the ring! That's where he'd learn a lot!"

"Are we going to be in our own weight division?" asked Sam, who weighted in as a lightweight at one hundred and thirty-three pounds.

"Pretty much," nodded Matt, "although we may have to do some shifting around so that everybody gets in several matches. There will be four different clubs there and each one will bring three to five fighters."

"Any real championships here?" asked Mark.

Matt shook his head. "Just good experience and a chance to see how your boys measure up. I'm excited, myself!"

"Are Fern and the girls going to go along?" asked Mark.

"Not this time, but Seth is planning on being there. We kind of need his help, although they will have people that can help out in a pinch."

"Do you do this often?" asked Bill. "I mean make trips to other places where you can have some different competition?"

"Yeah, we do," nodded Matt. "As much as we feel the need to do so."

"Where all do you go?" the boy asked.

"Colorado Springs, of course. Sometimes something comes up in Denver where we want to take part. Occasionally we go back to Wichita and sometimes we even get up to Kansas City."

At the mention of the last destination, a cloudy look passed over the face of the young boxer.

They boarded the train the following morning and were headed toward

Colorado Springs and Bill's first experience with other boxing clubs. The boy was excited.

"Don't you wish you were fighting instead of just standing around watching?" asked Mark. "A good fighter isn't content to just stand around."

"I believe a good fighter tries to do what his trainer wants him to do," replied Bill softly.

"Did you ever get into any scraps at school, Bill?" asked Mark as he dropped into a seat beside the young boxer.

Bill shrugged and then looked at the older fellow. "I guess the answer to that is what fellow hasn't?"

"Yeah, I'd expect," nodded Mark.

"Bill, you ever seen the mountains?" asked Matt, who along with Seth, had taken the two seats right in front of Mark and Bill.

"Oh, yeah," nodded Bill. "We've got some mountains back in Missouri and down in Arkansas."

"If those are the only ones you've seen," chuckled Matt, "You've got a surprise coming!"

When Captain Comet's Combat Club disembarked from the train at the Colorado Springs depot, Bill was still staring in disbelief at the huge range of Rocky Mountains looming in the west.

The team checked into the hotel not too far from the station and then walked on to the Spring House where the competition would be held over the next three days; Friday, Saturday and Sunday. They would do a little sightseeing and then catch the train back to Kansas on Tuesday morning.

At the Spring House, Matt's group was checked into one of the rooms that were normally reserved for athletic clubs checking in to take part in either competition or workout sessions. Here they stored their equipment so they didn't have to carry it back and forth from the hotel to the Spring House.

After getting established, the boys dressed out and went into the huge area where there were a number of rings. It seemed to Bill like there were hundreds of fighters working out. In addition to the local club and the three invited clubs, there were the many individual fighters who paid a fee to work out at the Spring House on a daily basis.

It wasn't long before Matt's club was in full swing and Bill soon realized he was huffing and puffing from the workout.

"I hadn't thought about it," said Matt to Bill, as the boy stopped to catch his breath, "but we're quite a bit higher in altitude out here. If you're not used to it, you really wear out quickly. The other boys have been out here enough that it doesn't bother them so much. Only in the late rounds!"

Later, Bill was aware that Matt was sitting off to one side with Seth and another fellow and they were really involved in something. And once in a while, one of them would throw a look toward the boy and he just had a feeling they were discussing him.

When the session was over, the club returned to their hotel where they cleaned up and went down to the cafeteria and the food bar where they could help themselves to whatever type of food they wanted to eat.

"We have a little news," said Matt, once they were all seated around their table. "This won't make Mark real happy, but I think the rest of you will be okay with it. I have intentionally left it as though Bill were not going to participate in any of the matches. I didn't want to stick him in with some experienced fighters and get the living daylights beat out of him. If I wanted that, I could always let Mark take another swing at him. But here is the mojo. There are some other fellows here that are in about the same boat as Bill, so we have arranged for Bill to be involved in a few bouts as well."

"How come you said that wouldn't make me real happy?" asked Mark, a frown on his face. "I been saying all along that Bill ought to be in the ring!"

"Because," said Matt and then he stopped. "In case you don't like what I am going to say, Mark, you are always free to pack up your duffle bag and move on. You don't fight well if you don't like the situation you are currently in. Now, the reason I said you wouldn't like this is, as everyone knows, you want to be the one to get in the ring and put the young upstart in his place! That is not how we produce fighters! First, you are older than Bill. Second, you are in a class higher because of weight, and third, you've had a lot more experience."

Everyone around the table was quiet and had stopped eating.

"I'd say, if you want to fight Bill, in a year or so, he will have gained some weight and some experience and then you might get a shot at him. But not right now."

Having nothing to add, the group went back to eating.

The first bouts the following day were scheduled for late morning. Unless agreed upon differently, there would be three rounds per fight with a one minute break between each round. In these matches, each round would go for two minutes since most of the boxers were of a younger age.

The Spring House was large and in the training area there were several rings. Generally there would be more than one fight going on at a time, however, a club usually only had one fighter going at it at a time. If there developed a conflict, they would hold up a fight until the problem had cleared.

Captain Comet's Sam Smith, also known as 'Smitty' in the boxing ring, had the very first fight on the card. He was matched up with a local boxer from Colorado Springs and the two young men looked to be cast from the same mold.

The fight went smoothly and Sam looked good as he fought. Matt Fenwick was very pleased with the outcome, especially after 'Smitty' was declared the winner.

Larry Lawrence was the second of Captain Comet's boys to enter the ring that morning. He was listed as 'The Fist' but no one ever called him that. Larry's bout went much the same as Smitty's had with the fundamentals looking very good. Matt was pleased although he disagreed with the decision going to the opposing boxer from Denver.

"Matt never agrees with the decisions that don't go our way," laughed Sam, who was standing beside Bill. "I don't know if he really disagrees, or if that is just his way of backing his own boxer."

"Yeah, Matt is very protective," Mark agreed. "Kind of like an old mother hen with her little chicks!"

Bill just happened to glance at Mark and realized the fellow was meaning him, that Matt was protecting him!

It shouldn't have, but that little jibe bothered Bill. He was not on the card for this morning, but he would be in the ring in the afternoon session.

"Bill," continued Matt, "I want you to move over to ring number three and watch those two boys. One of them will be your opponent sooner or later, perhaps both."

"Okay," nodded Bill, moving toward the ring where the two young men were getting ready to start their match.

Bill stood off to one side and watched the proceedings. After the first round, the young boy was sure he could beat either one of the two new guys in the ring. The excitement began to grow as he waited for his afternoon match.

"What do you think, Bill?" Sam inquired. "I think you are right there with either one of those guys."

"That is kind of the feeling I've got."

When the fight was over Bill and Sam both moved over to the ring where Mark was preparing to start his bout. The man from *Captain Comet's Club* exuded confidence, almost to the point of being cocky.

"Well, what did you think of the two boys in ring three?" asked Matt as he approached his boxers.

"I am ready to get in there with one of them," said Bill. "Can hardly wait!"

Mark 'the Masher' Milton, as he was listed on the card was ready to go and the fellows all turned their attention to the ring.

The bell rang and the fight was a flurry of swinging fists. Mark moved fluidly and easily with good footwork. He blocked everything the opponent threw at him.

Then suddenly there was a loud smack and Mark's opponent crumpled to the canvass and the Masher stepped back.

The fellow was sitting up, quite groggy, as the count reached ten.

"That sure was a quick fight," said Bill.

"Uh-huh," nodded Matt. "Not unlike Mark at all. He usually gets a knock-down somewhere along the line at every one of these practice sessions we go to."

Bill nodded . Suddenly he understood why Matt was so set against letting him and Mark get into it again! And also why it had bothered Mark so much! Bill knew he'd better be careful if he and Mark were to meet in a ring again.

It was two o'clock in the afternoon when Bill finally got his chance in the ring. His opponent was a tall rangy kid that appeared to have a long reach. He had come with the club from Grand Junction.

Matt, Seth, Mark, Sam and Larry were all ringside to see Bill's first effort in the ring. The building was stuffy, even with a great number of fans running. But that was due to the fact there were a great many boxers in the gymnasium and they were all sweating profusely at one time or another.

Matt had told Bill to just feel his opponent out the first round and get into blocking the punches. "Don't let him tag you," he had warned. "Move your feet. Bob and weave a lot, make him really have to work to get anything."

"Go get 'em, Stony!" came Seth's voice.

"Stony?" questioned Bill, surprise in his voice.

"Yeah, you are Bill 'Stony' Young on the fight card."

"Oh," the novice said as he turned and stepped into the ring.

Bill appeared to be somewhat shy in the ring. He easily fended off the punches thrown his way by the Grand Junction fighter. But there were openings he could have taken advantage of, but did not do so.

With the bell to end round one, Matt was in the ring and talking earnestly to his young boxer. Bill would occasionally nod, acknowledging the instructions of his trainer.

"Okay, Bill," Matt directed. "Get in there and take advantage of those openings!"

The second round was fifteen seconds underway when the opposing boxer landed a combination of punches that caused Bill to back pedal. Matt was shouting instructions when suddenly the hillbilly sent a right straight arm punch that caught the boxer square on the end and the chin. Lightning had struck.

For all practical purposes, the young fellow looked exactly like the antagonist that Mark had sent to the deck. The youngster landed hard but was never totally unconscious. He moved and tried to get his bearings but was only in a sitting position when he was counted out.

Bill went over to help the boy to his feet but the referee warned him back immediately. Surprised, Stony went back to his corner.

"Wow," exclaimed Mark, "you sure learn quick! I couldn't have done that any better myself!"

"We've got three out of four," said Seth. "We've scored two knockouts, won a decision and lost a decision that could easily have gone our way. We really can't complain too much!"

Sam Smith was the next fighter up and he easily won his match. He far outclassed his opponent.

Then came Larry Lawrence in a good solid slugging match. Larry knocked his man down twice in the third round and came away the winner.

Bill's second match gave him an opponent from Denver and this time he actually absorbed a few hits on the side of his head. Matt was talking almost continually to his young boxer, warning him not to let those punches land.

With about fifteen seconds left in the first round, Bill suddenly came alive with a series of power punches that had his opponent dazed as the bell sounded.

"They'll have him going again by the start of the round," said Matt, "but I think you could just go out there, take the fight to him and get it over with in this round."

They were ten seconds into the second round when Bill suddenly stepped in and a flashing straight jab connected with the chin of the Denver boxer. The fellow staggered backwards and went down, sprawling out on his back on the canvas.

"That was about the quickest punch I've seen a young fellow throw!" said Seth. "With a punch like that in your arsenal, you could handle about anybody! Of course, you need just a little bit of luck!"

Mark's match was the next to last match on the card for Friday. His opponent was a big boy from the Springs and the fellow was impressive. The Kansas boys had watched him in one of his earlier rounds and thought he might be up to giving Mark a good fight.

The two boxers would often stand toe to toe and pound each other until they were forced to break from a clinch. Both seemed to be able to absorb whatever the other one dished out.

At the end of round two, both boxers seemed somewhat weary. Both men had several bruises that were beginning to show on their faces. The first two rounds had been brutal.

"Mark," said Matt, just before the start of the third round, "just pretend that is Bill out there and see what you can get done! Okay?"

Mark gave a tired nod.

The round had just got underway when Mark feinted with a right jab and when his opponent reacted; the Mangler stepped in with a combination of hooks and jabs. The fellow was slow in covering up and a left cross connected solidly.

Mark's opponent staggered backwards, blood streaming from his hard hit nose. Then he sat down and the towel came in from his manager's corner. The fight was over.

It had been a full and hard day and *Captain Comet's Combat Crew* were extremely tired. They did not stay around to watch the final bout between a local boy and a boxer from Grand Junction.

The boys showered, went down to the cafeteria and were back in their rooms, asleep, in short order.

Matt and Seth were very excited over the success of their boxers and talked for a long time before turning in for the night.

●●●

Sam 'Smitty' Smith was the first of the Captain's boxers in the ring the following morning. He was paired against a fellow from Denver with the moniker 'Jasper One-Punch' and by the end of the first round: it was obvious he only had one punch. It was a wild jab that seldom made connection.

"Just don't get too confident," said Matt between rounds. "If he were to land a lucky one, it might be all over!"

"Should I try to take him out?" asked Sam.

"Only if the opportunity presents itself. Just don't get away from your game trying to get something spectacular, Sam," the trainer cautioned.

Halfway through the second round Smitty landed a very solid blow that sent his opponent to his knees. He was woozy getting up and the fight was called.

There was a time gap before either Bill or Larry were scheduled to fight in the welterweight division.

Larry 'the Fist' Lawrence stepped into the ring to face 'Bobcat' Jones in the next bout for the Captain's boxers. It was a tough match but Larry won on the decision.

Immediately 'Stony' Young was in the adjoining ring facing 'Hammer' Fredericks. The Denver boxer kept backing up from the very beginning. The fellow continued to bob and weave, constantly moving away from Bill as he back pedaled.

"He's afraid of you, Stony!" shouted Mark from the sidelines where the boxers from Kansas were gathered.

Bill quickened the tempo of his hits forcing the fellow to cover up and move quickly to escape the pounding he was taking.

Then came the opening and Bill's fist was like lightening as it connected with the point of the Hammer's chin. The boxer's knees buckled and he went down. The ten count came and went and the boy was still on his back. But his trainers had him up and moving about within another minute.

Mark 'the Mangler' was scheduled next in a different ring. He was paired against someone nicknamed 'Torpedo' but the name was the only thing he had in common with the military weapon.

Matt had told Mark to hold back and not try to KO any more boxers. "The thing is, we want to be invited back," the manager explained. "If you keep decking all your competition, they may think twice about asking us to return."

The boxer nodded. Then he turned back to the manager. "What about Bill?" he asked. "He has been knocking them down just as often as me."

"Yeah, I know," smiled Matt. "I'm going to speak to him as well. You fellows can both get in a lot of good work without having to lay anybody out."

"Okay," Mark acquiesced.

Mark followed his trainer's instructions. He moved quick and he forced the other fighter to fight his game. The Mangler made the other boxer look bad but he did not try to actually knock him down. Mark easily won the match.

Saturday afternoon was more of the same with all four of the Captain's boxers picking up wins. They were careful not to put anyone on the canvas.

It was late in the evening when Rowdy Jacobs, the fellow in charge of the boxing venue, came to see Matt Fenwick.

"Matt," he said, taking the promoter by the arm and leading him away from the ring, "I've got a situation I want to share with you."

"Yeah, what's up, Rowdy?"

"The fellow from Denver and the guy from Grand Junction came to see me together. Don't think they'd have had the nerve to come by themselves. But anyhow, they were complaining about two of your boys being too far advanced to be in this competition. I tried to explain that one of them was just a beginner. I don't think they believed me, though."

"I was afraid of something like this," Matt confessed.

"They said if I invited you fellows again, they'd just pack up and go home. They said they didn't need their young guys hammered around the way that Mark Milton and Bill Young can do it."

"I about have to take my full compliment of boxers," said Matt. "Not much benefit in just taking your bottom half. Those are the fellows that are probably never going to amount to much as a boxer."

"Right," Rowdy agreed. "But I do have a possible alternative for you," he grinned.

"And what's that?"

"Fellow from Kansas City called me a few days ago," said the Colorado Springs promoter. "He is getting a tournament lined up and wanted to know if I had any boxers that I felt would benefit in taking part. I told him maybe in six months, but not in a few weeks. I could get hold of him and see what slots are available, if you want."

"Yeah, I'd appreciate that," Matt smiled. "Could we call him right now?"

"Let's see if he's in." Rowdy led the way to his office.

Butch Bullfinch was indeed in his office and was very pleased to hear from Rowdy. He was also excited about the prospect of adding two new, unknown, boxers to his fight card. Before they were off the phone, Mark Milton and Bill Young had been added to the Mid America Boxing Challenge just two weeks down the road.

"Will we still be able to bring our boxers out here?" asked Matt as he and Rowdy returned to the rings.

"Once you have been in the level of tournament your two top boys are now in, they are no longer eligible for this kind of setup, Matt." replied Rowdy. "They can come along and help you out, but they can't actually get in the ring and box."

"Uh-huh," the promoter responded.

●●●

Matt Fenwick gathered together his boxers and they walked back to the hotel. Again, they showered and went down to the cafeteria for the evening meal.

"Boys," said the promoter, as they began finding their places around the table with plates of food, "I've got some news to share with you."

The boxers sat down quietly and began to eat as they listened to their manager. Matt explained the situation and that Mark and Bill had been entered in the Mid America Boxing Challenge in Kansas City just two weeks away.

"I plan to take all four of you," said the Fenwick, "although at the moment Mark and Bill are the only ones entered in the tournament."

"Do you think me and Larry could get in?" asked Sam.

"I don't know," replied Matt. "I will check that out, but I'm thinking we may have to try to find other matches there in Kansas City, if you are to box. Seth would have to go with you and I would stay at the Mid America location."

"What about tomorrow?" asked Mark. "Do me and Bill still have to hold off, or can we go to work on our opponents?"

"I'd like to say you need the practice for this upcoming tourney and to just go ahead and hammer 'em!" their trainer exclaimed. "But I think that is unsportsmanlike, plus Rowdy helped get you guys into that big tournament. We need to maintain a working relationship with the group out here."

Mark and Bill both nodded.

"We'll box tomorrow and I want you all to work on finesse. Consider it accelerated sparring; get in as much of a work out as you can against your opponent but don't just beat him to a pulp. That doesn't do him any good, nor does it really help us.

"On Monday, I think we will take a little trip up Pikes Peak! Ought to do that while we are out here. I understand the view is great up there! Then Tuesday morning we'll be on our way back east and some really intense training for those Mid America bouts!"

●●●

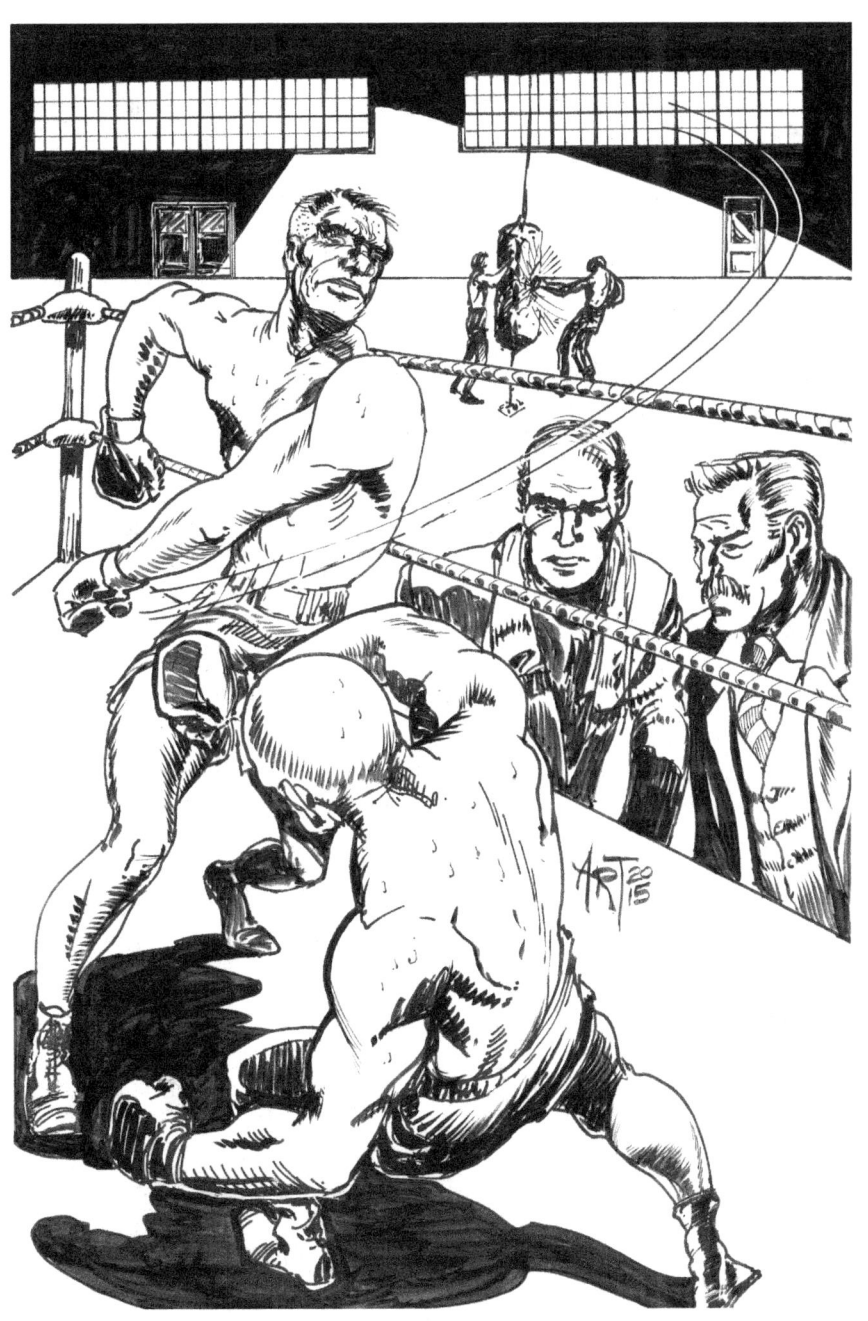

"Will we still be able to bring our boxers out here?

Sunday came and each fighter had one boxing match in the afternoon. Fenwick's boxers won all four easily.

"Matt," said Bill, as they returned to their hotel, "I know it has to cost a lot of money to run a boxing club and I am just wondering where you get the finances to take care of four boxers?"

"You know, Bill, you are the first boxer to ever ask me where the money comes from," chuckled the trainer. "And the answer is that we get a cut of the gate from events like this one right here. You get more if you win than if you bring in a bunch of losers."

"Were they charging to get in? I wasn't aware of it."

"Yep, they were, kid. A dollar a head per day. That was just to get in and walk around and look things over. Of course, there were usually some bouts going on somewhere, so you could really get your fill of boxing, if you wanted to!"

"I noticed there were a lot of people from Denver down here," Mark observed. "I'll bet they were following their boxers!"

"I expect they were," agreed Matt. "I saw a number from Grand Junction, but not nearly the amount that showed up from Denver."

"Where is Grand Junction?" asked Bill.

"West of Denver, clear across the state," Matt informed. "It was a good haul to get here."

"Were there any people from Kansas here?" Larry inquired.

"Probably," Matt continued, "but I didn't see any that I knew. None of you guys have parents or family in the area, so it wasn't likely we would have a following."

"Yeah, not much boxing going on in Kansas," Mark commented.

Captain Comet's Combat Club spent Monday on Pikes Peak and in the surrounding area. Then it was back to the hotel for a night's sleep before making the trip back to the flatlands of Kansas.

Matt Fenwick had picked up a copy of the Colorado Springs Evening Telegraph and was looking through the newspaper as the train pulled away from the depot.

"Bill," called Matt, when they were a short distance out of Colorado Springs, "there is a piece here in the paper you might be interested in. It is about a footrace up the mountain."

"The mountain? You mean Pikes Peak? How could they do that? We could hardly breathe up there!" Bill was curious.

"I think they all lived out here," Matt reasoned. "Says here twenty-five men and two women started the climb. Eighteen men and one woman finished it."

"Boy, I wonder how long it took 'em!" exclaimed Sam.

"It says here the first guy up took a little over three hours. It also says they followed some trail up the east face, so I'm guessing it wasn't as long as that automobile road we were on yesterday."

"I bet if a guy came out here and practiced it, he could do a decent job of getting to the top," Bill suggested with a faraway look in his eyes.

"Maybe we'll just have to come out here and train for a week," Fenwick thought aloud. "Kind of get in shape for the altitude, you know."

"You think they are going to run it again?" asked Bill.

"Who knows?" Matt went back to reading the paper.

●●●

If the boys from *Captain Comet's Combat Club* thought they had been training hard before, they got a real jolt the rest of the week. Matt and Seth both were working them like there was no tomorrow. When the day was over, they were totally exhausted.

Matt placed a call to the Mid America Boxing Challenge and talked to Butch Bullfinch, the man in charge of the tournament.

When Matt got off the phone with Bullfinch, he looked just a little bewildered.

"Are we gonna get in?" asked Larry.

"The same group that is doing the Mid America tournament is also doing a tournament across town for some of the lesser boxers in the area. He was a little reluctant, but finally said he would let Larry and Sam compete in that competition.

"He also told me what the entry fee was for each of the four boxers and it seemed a little bit on the exorbitant side to me. But I agreed that we would pay."

"I suppose they charge an admission fee, like they did at Colorado Springs," said Bill. "Maybe we get a cut of that."

"Yeah, they charge, but we don't get a cut of it. However, the prizes for winning are on the high side. But, in order for you to keep your amateur status, the winnings go to your club. The boxer just gets a medal."

"What do you mean by amateur status?" Bill scratched his chin.

"It means you don't box for money," Fenwick explained. "You box for the joy of boxing and because you like to compete. If you are to win an AAU Championship or if you make the Olympic team, you must be an amateur athlete.

"Also, I need to have publicity shots of each one of you taken and in to the Mid America Association just as soon as we can get it done. We'll catch a train to Pratt tomorrow and have it done over there. They have a very good photography shop."

"Hey, while we're there," grinned Bill, "I'd like to introduce you to a fellow I met there. He is the one that said I should look up Captain Comet. But he knew blessed little else about the Captain."

The following day they were in Pratt where they had the pictures made and the photographer promised he would have them finished and sent to Mid America the following day. The fellow was a little surprised when Matt Fenwick told him he would pay him when the photos arrived in time to be used by Mid America. And, at that point, he would pay him double.

The fellow again promised they would be on time.

They left the photography studio and Bill led the way across Main Street to a small smoke filled pool hall on the east side of the road. It was dark and dingy inside and the boy asked for the owner. The man behind the counter left, going back among the pool tables. Presently he was back with a small fellow in rumpled clothing. His dress didn't particularly look unclean, just rumpled.

When the little fellow saw Bill, he broke into a grin. "Gonna give me a chance to get my money back?"

"Howdy, Paddy," smiled Bill. "Yeah, I'd like to, but we don't have the time. However, I want you to meet Captain Comet, otherwise known as Matt Fenwick. Matt this is Paddy. I don't know his last name."

"I'd tell you my last name," said the little man as he reached out to shake hands, "but I don't know what it is either!" Then he laughed.

"When I first got into town, I stopped by here," Bill reported. "I sometimes engage in a game of pool to pick up a little cash. I played in here for several hours on that Friday."

"Any you fellows ever shoot pool with Bill?" asked Paddy, looking at the men accompanying the young fellow. As a group they shook their heads negatively.

"Then my advice is, don't! The kid is damn good! He'll clean you out!"

"Did he clean you out?" Mark wanted to know.

"Me and several other guys," Paddy chuckled. "Okay, you been warned. Now, what brings you back to Pratt?"

"I now belong to *Captain Comet's Combat Club*," said Bill. "We are in town to have photographs taken for some boxing matches we'll be competing in up in Kansas City."

"Can't you stay long enough for me to take a shot at getting some of my money back?" asked the pool hall owner.

"How about thirty minutes?" Bill turned to Captain Comet. "I am nearly broke!"

"One game," Matt relented. "Then we are on the train again."

"Two," Bill retorted. "Paddy will want a chance to win his money back and it's only sporting that I give him another chance."

"You'd better get to playing because the train doesn't wait on anyone!" grinned Matt.

The little old pool shark turned and made a mark on the calendar behind the counter.

"What did you just do?" asked Matt, out of curiosity.

"I marked that Bill was here to play pool!" the fellow said. "It's an event in this pool hall. I marked the last time he was here, too, 'cause he took so much from so many!" The guy gave a cackling laugh as he was in his element.

They played two games and it did not take very long either time. Bill won everything. The old timer was somewhat frustrated, but he knew what kind of player Bill was before they started. The two games drew a small crowd.

"We gotta go again," Paddy grumbled.

"Can't."

"Not fair! I need a chance..."

"From what I've seen," said Matt jokingly, "you fellows could play all night and it would still be the same! Now we gotta get to the depot!"

"I'll come back some time when I can stay longer," Bill promised Paddy, as the boxers filed out of the smoke filled pool hall.

"I wonder if he really didn't know his last name?" asked Sam.

"According to the framed liquor license hanging on the wall behind the cash register, his last name was Long," Fenwick contributed as they made for the train station.

●●●

The work continued.

Those sandy roads south of the great bend in the Arkansas River provided some tough footing for training and Matt Fenwick took full advantage of it.

With the heavy workouts, the time flew and they were soon looking to board the train to Kansas City.

They were met at the depot by a representative of the Mid America Boxing Challenge and taken directly to their hotel which was within walking distance of the boxing venue.

Bill, who was new to all of the activities around boxing, was glad for the experience in Colorado Springs. The scene was not quite as mind boggling as it might have been. They spent some time just looking over the surrounding area and the gym where the competition was to be held.

Almost before he knew it, Bill was preparing for his first match. Here, they were being introduced to a large crowd of spectators over a loud speaker.

Then, almost in a daze, Bill heard the bell and he was in the first round of his fight. He listened to Matt who talked to him as he went through the motions of boxing. With the end of the first round, Matt was right in his young boxer's face, reading him a riot act!

It seemed to bring Bill out of his daze and shortly into the second round, he caught his opponent with a short hook that sent him to the canvass. The fellow was immediately up on one knee where he took and eight count.

Thirty seconds later, the lightning in Bill's glove struck and the man staggered back and then went down. He did not come up on his knee this time.

A short time later, Mark won his bout by decision, although it was not close.

The following morning, Sam and Larry, accompanied by Seth Harkins, left for the venue some distance away where they would compete.

Mark and Bill both fought in the morning and both won by decisions. They were scheduled to fight again in the afternoon. At this point, Matt was very pleased with his two talented fighters.

The late afternoon matches drew huge crowds and Bill didn't think he'd ever seen so many people in one place.

His opponent in the third match came at him hard and quick. Generally there is a bit of time in which the two fighters feel each other out, but it seemed like this fellow wanted to get it over with quickly. Bill obliged when the fellow left his chin unguarded for a split second. The glove was there so quick the fellow did not know what hit him. It was like a shot of electricity and the fight was over with a first round knock-out.

"Wow!" gasped Mark. "You really tagged him, Bill!"

"Yeah, he left himself wide open."

"You've had three bouts and two KO's," Mark reminded his friend. "You are going to be the one they are pointing for, Bill! You better be ready!"

Mark won his bout and they returned to the hotel. They had not been there long when the door opened and Sam and Larry piled into the room.

"We both won!" exclaimed Sam. "How'd you guys do?"

The four boxers sat and talked for a while before going to eat and then to bed.

●●●

The following day found the competition to be somewhat stronger and it took all Bill and Mark had to come out on top. But they managed to win their bouts. They would now be in the championship rounds.

Sam and Larry were also in the championship rounds over in the junior tournament. Everything seemed to be going great for the Captain Comet boxers. Yet, Matt Fenwick knew, it is when all is going perfectly, that something unexpected happens. He just hoped it wasn't this time!

The evening of the title fights was cloudy and cool for what had been a series of very hot days in the Kansas City area.

Matt Fenwick wondered if the heat in the earlier matches might have been an advantage for his fighters as they had been training in some sweltering temperatures. But there was not a thing he could do about the weather.

Pre-fight introductions were made and Bill 'Stony' Young had difficulty believing all the hype he was hearing was about him. However, when he listened to the introduction of Red 'the Spike' Brubaker, he wondered how he was supposed to defeat someone of that caliber.

Bill was knocked to the mat just twenty seconds into the first round. He shook his head and got to one knee, waiting for the mandatory eight count. Then he was up and the fight resumed with Bill thinking if it came down to a decision, he would lose because of that knock down. He could hear Matt, far away, yelling instructions but he couldn't really understand his trainer with all the noise in the building.

They were down to the final seconds of the first round when Bill got in a hard uppercut that lifted Spike off the floor and he went down just as the round ended.

Matt realized Bill was a little woozy yet from that first knock down and had him breathe deeply of the smelling salts. They seemed to revive the kid.

"With that last punch, I figure the score is about even," Matt yelled loudly to be heard. "But Spike is local, so he probably has the edge here. Can you turn that lightning loose?"

The trainer was getting out of the ring and did not hear Bill's murmured reply. "Yeah, I can do that."

The second round was steady hard boxing and it looked like either fighter could win the bout. There were no knock downs in the second round.

"I think he is getting winded," said Matt. "I'm expecting him to come out and clinch a lot in an effort to save strength. Be careful and don't let him slip one in on you!"

Bill nodded.

Matt's prediction proved true as Spike tried to keep the fighting in close where he could grab the opponent. Bill continued to bob and weave trying to avoid the clinch.

Then Bill unleashed a combination of punches that staggered Spike. The boy stepped back and then when Spike lurched forward, he stepped in to meet him with another quick combination. But this time it ended with a quick jab that connected solidly on Red Brubaker's chin.

Spike's knees buckled and he was out before he hit the canvas.

Bill 'Stony' Young was the Welterweight Champion!

•••

There was a crowd of reporters around Bill Youngstone as he made his way back to the training room accompanied by Matt, Seth, Larry and Sam.

He was exhausted and every question that was put to him by the reporters was answered by Matt or Seth.

"How'd you guys do?" Bill asked in a raspy voice, looking at Sam.

"We both won," grinned Larry. "We had some good fights, but we came out on top."

"All that training we been doing," groaned Bill.

Mark's fight was about to start and the room cleared out. "Just rest," Matt said to his champion as he shooed everyone out of the room. "Let your body recuperate, son."

Bill lay back and let his eyes close.

The next thing he knew, Mark was back in the room with all the followers and reporters. He had just won the Middleweight Championship.

•••

Captain Comet's group was outside the boxing venue, waiting on a street corner to cross on their way back to the hotel.

"Matt Fenwick!" a loud authoritative voice shouted out. The group turned to see two well dressed men approaching.

"Yeah?" Fenwick replied.

"We need to talk to you for a few minutes."

"What about? This is hardly the place for a chat. Let's go into the hotel lobby over there. Be a lot more comfortable."

"Sure thing, Mr. Fenwick, lead on."

Bill noticed that two more men had joined the group from the opposite direction, making a total of four strangers.

When they gathered in the lobby, Bill found himself surrounded by the four men.

"Bill Youngstone," said the man who seemed to be in charge. "We are arresting you for the murder of Hap Ballenger down in Hollister last month!"

The group stood in shocked silence as the handcuffs were placed on Bill's wrists.

"We need to see some identification," demanded a much agitated Matt Fenwick.

All four of the men showed badges.

"I haven't killed anybody," said Bill.

"The courts will decide that," one of the coppers countered.

"You are saying I killed Hap Ballenger? When did I do this?"

"Don't be a smart aleck, boy! You killed him Friday evening, June fifth. There were witnesses."

"We're taking your boy downtown to the lockup," said one of the other men. "By this time tomorrow, we'll have him back in the Taney County jail!"

The four officers escorted Bill out of the hotel and into a waiting police car.

Captain Comet's group hustled to their room and cleaned up. Then they caught a cab to the police station where they were allowed to visit with their colleague.

"Glad to see you guys," Bill greeted them. "Congratulations on your title, Mark! You deserve it!"

"Bill," Matt Fenwick looking him straight in the eyes. "Did you kill that guy?"

"Of course not!" the boy scoffed. "Now, here is the thing. I was playing pool in Pratt with Paddy Long on Friday evening, the fifth of June. Paddy's got it marked on his calendar and you saw it there! Paddy is proof that I couldn't have been in Hollister at the time of this murder."

"Oh God, I'd forgotten about that, kid. You're right. No wonder you're not rattled being in the hoosegow. That sure is a relief. Last thing I want is to lose my new champion."

"Ha, no chance of that happening," Bill patted Fenwick on the arm. "I'm getting to like this boxing thing."

At that everyone bust out laughing.

"We'll get Paddy and be in Hollister about a day after they get you there," said Seth. "I'm on my way now!"

Their time was up and they left the police station with the feeling this would all be over soon and they could get back to training.

Matt Fenwick wondered; *things don't always turn out the way you think they will!*

THE END

WHY HILLBILLY LIGHTNING?

I had been thinking of writing a sports story for Airship 27's Sports Anthology, but I thought I would do one involving cross-country runners being involved in one of those things they used to do way back when. Something long and involved, like a footrace between Kansas City and Denver. Well, it was just a thought!

Then the Airship27 editor told me they really needed a boxing story, if I wanted to try one and that is how this one came about.

Now there are several incidents in the story that are based on fact. The first one involves the boy cutting a branch off a cherry tree so he can sit in the shade and eat cherries. That ruined the branch for ever producing more cherries, but what the heck. My granddad was the fellow who chased him off the farm! Yeah, it really happened.

The second incident that was real was the June 28, 1936 footrace up the east face of Pikes Peak. Our character, Bill, kind of wanted to run that, if they had it again the next year. This was the precursor of the Pikes Peak Marathon which is contested yearly. However, there was a twenty year gap from the first race before it was contested again in 1956. What is odd is the fact that the 1936 winner also competed in the 1956 event!

The third location that really existed was the old smoke filled pool hall in Pratt, Kansas, although all other facts about it are fictitious.

I hope you enjoy the story and won't be too harsh on me if I goofed up somewhere.

•••

JOHN R. ROSE is a fellow who seems to have been involved in sports of some kind throughout most of his life. That began with his enrollment into high school when the school principal asked if he was going out for football and he said "no." Then a voice behind him, said, "Yeah, he's going out." That was his dad speaking.

This was back at a time when there were no sports in the grade schools, or perhaps they played a little basketball during the winter months, but nothing really organized. So he didn't really know anything about the sports. If fact, he missed the first week of football practice because he had no clue they started practice before school started. He probably had a note somewhere that told him, but he hadn't bothered to read it.

Once started, he played football, basketball and ran track all through high school. those were the only sports offered. Later, after getting his teaching degree from Fort Hays State University, he coached at various times football, basketball (boys and girls), track (boys and girls) cross-country and volleyball. He spent over twenty years hosting and promoting Junior Olympic and Age Group Track & Field for boys and girls.

When attending national track meets where other sports were included, he often went to the boxing venue and watched the fighters. He does not claim to know anything about coaching the sport in any way!

The old coach now spends his time at the keyboard writing stories. His areas of interest include westerns, science fiction, jungle and, of course, sports.

SWITCH

by

Fred Adams, Jr.

"Let me get this straight," George McClannahan said around the stub of his cigar. "We win the game and we get fifty bucks?" He eyed the black man on the other side of his desk in the office of McClannahan's Hardware Store with skepticism.

Pearly Stubbs gave McClannahan the grin that earned him his nickname. His white teeth flashed in a con artist's smile that could sell a Grammaphone to a deaf man. "Yessir. That's a fact, and I have it right here."

Stubbs reached into the breast pocket of his brown mohair suit and ceremoniously took out a fifty dollar bill. He held it by the edges with his thumbs and forefingers to display as if it were a Rembrandt painting or a holy relic. "There she be." He snapped the bill for emphasis. "And it's yours if you beat us."

"And if you win, we don't pay you anything?"

"That's a fact. We use your field, we pass the hat to the crowd, and everybody has a good time."

"Just a regular nine-inning baseball game?"

"With a few concessions on the rules."

"What concessions?"

"You never heard of the Moline Wizards before, did you?"

"Can't say as I have."

"We're what you call barnstormers. We travel around from place to place to play ball, and we, shall I say, put on a show to entertain the crowd."

"What kind of show? Like a carnival?"

"More like a rodeo." Stubbs pulled out a handbill and slid it across George's desk. The handbill proclaimed the Moline Wizards would take on local teams in Topeka over a five-day stretch. "Watch the Wizards work magic on the diamond," it read. "See Home Run Harris knock five in a row over the wall. See Coley 'The Switch' Jackson strike out two batters at once. Can your team beat the Wizards?"

George's left eyebrow went up as the right one lowered. "To me you guys look like poolroom hustlers."

Stubbs's face slid from affable to hurt. "I'm insulted, Mr. McClannahan. If we were hustlers, we wouldn't tell you up front what we can do: win. Let alone print it on a handbill. Tell you what. I'll sweeten the pot. We'll spot you three runs."

"I don't know about this."

"Don't tell me you's a-skeered," Stubbs said, slipping into a minstrel show accent, "that the Whitlatch Tornadoes might lose to a bunch of down home colored boys." Stubbs's grin returned like a magic trick and once again he displayed the fifty dollar bill. "Fifty dollars." His eyebrows raised and voice lowered in a conspiratorial tone. "And if your team wins, I give you this fifty dollar bill. What you do with it is your business."

McClannahan turned his cigar between his thumb and forefinger, staring at it and thinking things over. His eye kept drifting to the bill. Finally, he put the cigar back in his mouth. "Spot us three runs, huh?"

"Yessir," Stubbs said.

"Okay, boy, you got yourself a game."

Pearly smiled even more broadly. "Now let's talk about those rules."

Out on the street Jefferson Smith saw Pearly coming up the sidewalk and climbed out of the rickety Model T. The wizened man hitched up his suspenders and walked around to the front of the car to crank the engine. He knew better than to ask questions before the clatter of the engine drowned out the conversation for passersby.

The pair climbed into the old coupe and Jefferson said, "Well?"

"He went for it, Jeff. He was a little tougher than most of 'em, but I got us a game for Saturday."

"I don't know how you talk them into it," Jeff said, pulling the car away from the curb.

"Curiosity, greed, and pride. Works every time. They just can't help themselves."

As they rode out of Whitlatch, they passed the Tornadoes' baseball field. Jeff said, "I checked it out. Grass is dry, hard ground, lots of bounce; not too rocky on the infield and the fence is only about three hundred twenty feet from the plate at the score board. Harris'll have no trouble hitting homers over that one."

"No bleachers. That's good. We'll sell all the traveling seats." In the equipment trailer the team carried folding chairs that they positioned along the base lines from home plate and rented out for ten cents. After giving away free seats to the mayor, the sheriff and a few local dignitaries, they could usually count on at least five bucks a game.

"Let's get back to Campion and give the team the good news."

Coley Jackson dozed in the late afternoon shade, leaning against the rear wheel of the bus, his glove behind his head as a pillow. A horse fly landed on the back of his left hand and before it could bite him, Coley's right hand swooped in and closed on the offending insect. He turned his fist thumb up and opened it. Before the fly could buzz away, Coley's hands clapped together with a sharp crack.

"He ain't gonna bite nobody no more, man or horse." Coley said.

"How you do that, Switch?" said Tory Bagley. The chunky catcher wiped his brow with the back of his wrist.

"You put your hand where the fly's gonna be, not where you see him." Coley grinned. He added, "Plus you gotta be fast."

"You oughta be in center field, not on the pitcher's mound."

"Too far to walk."

"Hey, here come Pearly and Jeff."

The Model T wheezed and clattered through the gate into the pasture where the team bus was parked. Jeff and Pearly got out and Jeff whistled between his fingers. One by one nineteen black men filed out of the bus or rose from their blankets to stand in a ragged knot in front of their manager.

"Here's the news." Jeff was only five-foot-six, but when he addressed the team, his in-charge demeanor made him seem taller than the tallest among them. "We play Saturday in Whitlatch. Pearly and I are still looking for a team to play on Sunday, but Saturday's on for sure. The bus ain't going into town Friday because I want you all sharp for Saturday, but tonight," he shrugged, "Amos'll take you into Rockland for a little R and R."

This news was met with grunts of approval, "Yeahs," "Okays," and "All rights."

"So let's put up the tent."

Jeff started using the old war surplus barracks tent years before because he got tired of the indignity of being turned away by whites-only hotels and boarding houses in the small towns where they played their games. Besides, once he bought the tent, it didn't cost him cash out of pocket every night of the week. There were nights when they'd all sleep on the bus while Amos drove to some town to play the next day, but every chance they got, the team would pitch the tent in some field and spend the night sleeping prone, not bent in half on a hard-backed seat.

Pitching the tent became a communal ritual that included every man on the team, Amos, Pearly and Jeff himself, a bonding rite that erased the line between labor and management, rookies and long-timers. Jeff had been in the game a long time and understood the value of camaraderie.

"We gonna be brothers," he told the team. "We play together, we work together, we eat together, we sleep together and we shit together. Ain't no stars on this team. The team is the star."

Once the tent was up, the players cleaned up and dressed up for a night on the town. They'd been to Rockland before and especially favored a juke joint near the freight terminal called Etta Mae's. The food was good, the drinks were cheap, and there was always a hot band playing.

Switch sat at a table with Tory, Elmo Bright, Benny Torrance, and the new kid Billy Potts. The band, a bass, drummer and piano backed a guitarist who wore his instrument almost at his knees. Lonnie Blunstone played and sang the blues with the best of them and tonight made his guitar laugh, cry, and quote the Holy Scriptures. The packed dance floor swayed to his rhythms like tides in the ocean. The heat, the smoke, and the crush of bodies wound the room like a spring.

"Damn, that dude can play," said Tory, around a mouthful of beans and pork, pointing with his fork at the bandstand.

"Everybody got a gift," said Elmo. "Ain't that what Jeff always says?"

"Guess what hers is," Benny said. He pointed a dark-skinned beauty in a slinky flower print dress sashaying across the dance floor.

She looked back at Switch and smiled through the haze of smoke, enjoying his stare. He raised his glass in salute and nodded. She turned away but in a second stole a glance over her shoulder to see if he were still looking. Then she gave her game away by looking past Switch to the far end of the room.

"You oughta go get you some of that, Switch" said Benny. "She's eyeing you up like a cat and a catfish."

"Two minutes into negotiation, I'd be negotiating with that big fish at the end of the bar. Man looks like a gorilla in a suit. She's been hanging on his arm for the last hour." A broad shouldered giant, neck too thick to button his collar, stood with his foot on the rail and a highball glass lost in his paw of a hand.

"Might almost be worth it," said Benny.

Switch shook his head. "She likes the idea men fight over her. Woman like that get a good man killed. Plenty enough peaches on the low limbs."

"Who's that dude coming over here?" said Billy.

Switch looked across the floor. "Oh, hell. Here comes Dobie."

A short man in a shiny blue suit with Switch's face but conked hair and a thin line of moustache slithered through the dancing couples and dropped into an empty chair at Switch's table. "Hey, big brother."

Switch eyed him with less than enthusiasm. "Hey, little brother. What you doing here?"

Dobie grinned. "Just passing through and I saw your bus outside. Can't drive by without saying hello."

"I thought you were working some big deal in Saint Louis, Dobie," Tory said.

"Oh that fell through, so I'm headed east. Got me a line on something good in Cleveland."

"You look prosperous enough," said Elmo. "Buy us a round."

"I ain't got a lot of spare cash. Don't you read the newspapers? There's a Depression going on."

"Wouldn't know it by us," said Benny, "Living can't get much lower than scraping it outa the bottom of the bucket every day. And I lived like that since before the Depression."

That made the whole table laugh. Dobie put a cigarette in his mouth and pulled out a shiny gold lighter. "I'm'a tell you boys something. There's always money to be made. You just gotta — Hel-lo, angel." He rose from the table staring at the woman in the flowered dress. Switch was about to warn him off, but at that moment the band ended a song with a fevered crescendo and the crowd roared its approval.

Dobie caught the woman in the flowered dress by the elbow and whispered in her ear. She turned her head and gave him a smile full of teeth like the face of Death. Switch looked to the corner of the room and saw the big man step away from the bar. He rose from his chair. "Here it comes."

Dobie was too busy eyeing up the woman to see her beau shoving his way across the room toward him. A hand the size of a plate clamped on his throat. "What you doin' with my woman, boy?" He was as dark as a walnut and his face glowed in the neon bar lights like a fresh shoeshine. The band stood still like the rest of the room, holding their breath.

Dobie's eyes bulged. He tried to say something but couldn't get the air out. His hand slipped into his pocket and Switch saw him pull out a razor. He came up beside Dobie and his hand clamped on his brother's wrist. He dug a thumb into the nerves behind the joint and Dobie dropped the razor. Jeff kicked it across the floor toward his table where Elmo scooped it up like a grounder and slid it into his pocket.

Switch stared into the big man's face and said simply. "Let my brother go. He didn't know no better."

The big man turned his head to glare at Switch. "When I'm done with him, I'm gonna kick your ass too."

"Then you're gonna have to kick mine, boy." The voice came from behind Switch. Jeff walked around him and glared up into the giant's face. The big man stared at the wizened little man in disbelief, startled by the authority in his voice.

"And mine."

"And mine."

The bully looked around him and saw he was surrounded by Pearly and the team.

"Now you let that man go," Jeff said. "And next time, you don't want dogs sniffing 'round your woman, don't trot her out like breeding stock."

As if a gear turned in his head, the big man let go of Dobie and backed away, dragging the pouting woman with him. He turned his back and Lonnie Blunstone took his cue, launching into a loud bluesy riff. The band followed his lead and kicked into a raucous barrelhouse tune. Dobie raised his chin defiantly and got as far as, "That's right jive-ass," before Switch clamped his hand over Dobie's face, fingers digging into his cheeks like he was gripping a baseball. Dobie stumbled backward as Switch steered him through the tables and out the door into the parking lot.

Switch shoved him away and Dobie fell, sitting down hard in the gravel. "I promised Mama before she died that I'd watch out for you, but you just about run out that string, Dobie. What you think you was gonna do with that razor? You never cut nobody in your life. He'da took that blade off you and carved his name in your ass with it."

"Coley, I…"

"Get away from here while you're breathing. And next time, think again before you play Romeo at some strange piece of tail. Cleveland ain't the sticks, Dobie, and I ain't gonna be there to save your sorry ass."

Dobie opened his mouth to speak but changed his mind. He picked himself up from the gravel and slunk away, disappearing among the rows of cars.

Tory came out. "Is he gone?"

"He's gone. What's happening inside?"

Things're copacetic. Pearly just bought the big man and his date a drink and told them some jokes. They're all laughing like long lost friends."

Switch stared across the parking lot. "What do you do with somebody like Dobie?"

"Pray he lives long enough to grow up."

"I ain't holding my breath."

As the men got on the bus to ride back to their camp, Switch pulled Jeff aside. "Thank you for backing my play. I didn't know what I was gonna do next."

"If you think I'm gonna let my money-makers get busted up in a bar fight, you're crazy. Get on the bus." As Switch climbed the steps, Jeff took one last look around the lot and reached under his shirt to let the hammer down on the pistol in his waistband.

Friday was rain from start to finish, but the sun rose bright and hot on Saturday. Jeff and Pearly hadn't found a match for Sunday, but they decided to leave the tent standing and stay one more night.

The game was at one. Jeff told the Wizards to suit up at nine. The uniforms, tattletale grey flannel with red trim were castoffs from the Moline Badgers that Jeff bought for next to nothing and had his nieces Shondra and Betty patch and alter. Up close they looked rag-tag, but from the stands, they looked as good as new.

No names on the backs of the collarless shirts, just numbers because people came and went, but every uniform had an embroidered W over the heart, a Moline M that Jeff's nieces removed and sewed back on upside down. The trousers bloused out so wide that Tory once quipped he had to take two steps before the cuffs moved, which was incorrect, of course, because the shin-high cuffs were banded with rubber.

Pearly suited up too; he stepped out of the tent wearing a full tuxedo with tails. He carried a megaphone to work the crowd in one hand and a tall silk hat in the other. Once, when Elmo told him he looked like a high-priced pimp in his outfit, Pearly hit back with, "Then you's the whores, 'cause that's what I'm selling."

When the bus pulled up at the field, the other team hadn't arrived but the crowd had, curious to see what the Wizards could do. As they filed off the bus, Jeff said, "Get out there and warm up. Show 'em a little, but don't give it all away." Amos had to shoo a few non-payers from the chairs, but most of the spectators coughed up a dime with no protest. After all, the show was free.

The Wizards were all but through their warm-up drills when the Tornadoes pulled up in a caravan of eight gleaming automobiles and pickup trucks. They swaggered to their dugout to the cheers of the locals. Their blue and white uniforms, player names on the backs, looked as if they'd just come out of the box.

"Shiny cars, shiny shoes, shiny bats," said Petey Hobbes, the right fielder. "And they call us shines." Everybody laughed.

"Looks to me like that team's a rich man's hobby," said Jeff, squinting in the sun. "Probably McClannahan's."

The hardware store owner was the last to step onto the field, dressed in

Pearly stepped out of the tent wearing a full tuxedo with tails.

the same uniform as the players. The back of his shirt sported his name and below it the word Manager.

The Tornadoes were all white; that upped the ante for the crowd, which looked to be about half and half. The three umpires arrived in a separate car. Jeff would have worried if they rode in with the team, but after discussing the nature of the game and the variations on the rules with them, he believed they'd give the Wizards a square deal.

McClannahan surprised Jeff when the Tornadoes won the coin toss and chose the field first. He offered his hand to him. Jeff shook it, and George said, "Let's give them a good game."

Jeff smiled. "Yes, indeed." Back at the dugout, Jeff gathered the team around him. "Word is these boys're tough, but I say you're tougher. Get out there and prove me right."

A big woman in a long green dress and a straw hat as big around as a parasol sang "The Star Spangled Banner," with a voice like an ambulance siren, and the crowd rose to its feet. Women and children, men in suits and men in overalls, black and white alike took off their hats and held them over their hearts and sang along. Then Max Hayes the head umpire shouted, "Play Ball."

The Wizards' dugout was along the third base line, and Jeff stood at the spot where he would stay for the rest of the game, two-thirds of the way between home plate and third base where he could see every one of his players, and they could all see him.

The show didn't start until the second inning. Neither side had brought a man home, but the score board showed three-nothing for the Tornadoes, the runs the Wizards spotted the home team. The Wizards came to bat and first up was Petey. He came from the dugout twirling his bat like a baton. As he approached the batter's box, like a drum major, he threw it spinning high into the air.

The umpire jumped back and the catcher cringed and covered his head. Petey caught the bat one-handed as he nonchalantly stepped to the plate. The crowd laughed and cheered as Petey tipped his hat, tapped home plate a few times and took his stance. The Tornadoes' pitcher, Iron Mike Paterson, struck Petey out with two curves and a change-up, but it was not Iron Mike, it was Petey the crowd was applauding, delighted by his antics as Petey bowed from the waist and waved to them striding back to the dugout whistling and twirling his bat.

From the sideline, Pearly egged the crowd on. "How about it, ladies and gentlemen? Let's hear it one more time for Petey Hobbes." They clapped and cheered anew. Pearly all but had them in his pocket already.

As the Tornadoes came in from the field, Iron Mike passed Switch on his way to the mound and said, "I never saw a glove like that one, six fingers."

Switch grinned. "Truth be told, it's four fingers and two thumbs. Fits either hand."

"Whattaya call that?"

"You might call it ambidextrous. I call her Clarice."

One of the rules the Tornadoes agreed to suspend was the requirement that the pitcher declare right-handed or left-handed and stick with it the whole game. Switch threw three balls to the second batter after striking out the first, and Pearly called from the sideline, "Switch's getting tired. You folks wanna see him pitch lefty for a while?"

The crowd yelled its approval, and Switch held his hands over his head and with great ceremony took his glove from his left hand and put it on his right. Then he struck the batter out with the next three pitches.

At the end of the third inning, no runs had scored, and the game was still three-nothing. Time for some show. Pearly swaggered out halfway to the pitcher's mound with his tuxedo, and raised his megaphone. "Ladies and gentlemen, while the teams enjoy a brief time out, please allow me to introduce to you the Moline Wizards' second baseman, the amazing Tommy Troy."

Tommy was a tall lean man with long, spidery fingers. He ran from the dugout waving to the crowd. As he passed home plate, baseballs appeared in his hands and he began to juggle three of them as he trotted up the first base line, throwing one out of three behind his back over his shoulder to the delight of the crowd. As he passed first base, one of the Wizards threw him another ball and he juggled four as he ran to second where another ball was thrown to him from the sidelines. Tommy caught the fifth ball and put it into the rotation as he headed to third and a sixth ball was tossed to him.

He stood at home plate juggling all six baseballs and one by one threw them to his teammates in the dugout. When he was down to two, he juggled the pair one-handed then flung both high into the air. He caught the first in his cap and the second in his oversized pocket.

"How about that, folks?" Pearly shouted through the megaphone. "Ain't he something? Tommy Troy!" The crowd cheered and whistled. Tommy waved and trotted back to the dugout. He was the free token to get the crowd wanting more. Next time, Pearly would start passing the hat.

At the end of five, neither team had scored a run and the Wizards were still down by three. The hometown crowd was stoked. Switch stayed on the mound while the rest of the team went in. Pearly stepped out again. "Ladies and Gentlemen, please allow me to introduce The Moline Wizards' batting sensation, Home Run Harris!

"Folks, do you want to see Home Run Harris hit five in a row over the center field fence?" The response was mild, so Pearly said, "That's no Whitlatch answer. You want to see five in a row?"

This time the crowd responded with shouts and whistles. Harris stepped up the plate and after a few warm up swings nodded to Switch who threw a slider to Tory. Harris's bat connected with a crack like a gunshot and the ball sailed high over the fence. Switch's second pitch was low and outside, but Harris connected with another clean hit; home run number two. Harris knocked three, four and five out of the park.

The crowd applauded, but a voice called out, "He's throwing easy ones. Let Iron Mike pitch to him." Nobody noticed that it was Amos who protested. The crowd caught the fever and began to chant, "Iron Mike, Iron Mike." Harris looked to Jeff, who waited a three-count then nodded. The crowd went crazy as Iron Mike swaggered to the mound.

"Let's sweeten this a deal a little," said Pearly to the crowd. "We're gonna pass the hat while Iron Mike warms up, and the proceeds go to Harris if he hits five in a row, and if he doesn't, Iron Mike gets the money. Whaddaya say, folks?" Amos and Petey worked the baselines passing the hat. People threw in pennies and nickels, sometimes a dollar bill. The hats were jingling when they came back to home plate.

Iron Mike threw a blistering fast ball. Harris swung and missed. There were some hoots and boos from the crowd, but mostly cheers for the hometown hero. Paterson's second throw was a curve ball that dipped under Harris's bat. Strike two. The jeers were drowning out the applause now.

Someone shouted, "It's over. Get the bum outa there."

"Now wait a minute, people," said Pearly. "The deal was five in a row. Nobody says they have to be the first five."

Harris tapped his bat on the plate and took his stance. The chanting was louder. "Iron Mike. Iron Mike."

Iron Mike wound up and threw a slider to the outside. Harris stepped into the plate and swung. The ball soared over the scoreboard. Harris held up one finger to the crowd.

The next two flew easily over the fence, and Iron Mike's scowl was visible all the way to the dugout. He fired a fastball to the inside and this time, Harris edged back. The bat connected and the ball soared away. Harris held up four fingers.

Now the crowd was chanting, "Home Run. Home Run."

Iron Mike threw another fast ball, low and inside. Harris took a hard cut at it, and when he hit the ball, the bat split in his hands. The crowd held its breath as the ball flew in a low trajectory and hit the top of the fence, bouncing over it into the hands of the kids Jeff paid a penny a ball for shagging fouls and homers.

The crowd roared as Home Run Harris took his victory lap around the bases, hat in the air with one hand and five fingers in the air with the other.

"That was close," Elmo said.

Petey chuckled. "Close don't matter long's it goes over the fence."

If Iron Mike was rattled by the incident, it didn't show in his pitching. In the next inning he struck out two of the Wizards before and one after Elmo hit a bouncing single into right field.

Switch was alternating innings, pitching left-handed then right to keep the batters off balance, and the strategy worked. The best the Tornadoes got was a double after a strike out and a pop fly that shortstop Ollie Burke caught in his hat, bobbled in the air then snatched with his glove.

At the end of the seventh, Switch stayed on the mound; it was his turn in the spotlight. Pearly strutted out to the batter's box with two of the Wizards in tow, Jammy Carter and Bill Capp, bats over their shoulders. "Folks," he brayed through his megaphone, "all this fine afternoon you been enjoying the pitching skills of the one and only Switch Jackson. Let him know how much you appreciate him." The crowd clapped and whistled.

"And now," you're about to see another phenomenon. The amazing Switch is going to strike out two batters at once." He waved the batters to the plate, and they stood facing each other about ten feet apart. "Right before your very eyes, he's going to strike out one batter with his left hand and one with his right."

Bill was a lefty and Jammy right-handed, so when they took their stances they faced each other. "Okay, Switch," shouted Pearly. "Show 'em how it's done."

Switch held his bare hands over his head and rotated full circle to show the crowd a ball in each. He toed the rubber, and snapped a curve with his right hand to Jammy and within a second threw a slider to Bill. Both swung hard and the bats swished through the empty air.

"Stee-rike one," Pearly called out. "Let's make it interesting, Switch." To the crowd: "You wanna see him throw cross hand, right to left and left to right?" The crowd yelled its approval. "You heard 'em Switch."

Switch wound up again and this time threw with his right hand to Bill and his left to Jammy, the second throw coming so close after the first that the balls nearly collided halfway to the batters. Jammy swung and missed again, but Bill caught his pitch with the tip of his bat, sending it foul over the crowd and into the pasture beyond.

"Strike two! Now, folks, watch as Switch finishes off both batters by pitching both hands at once. Show 'em, Switch."

Switch took a long pause, his left toe on the rubber, then sent sidearm pitches with both hands at once. Both batters swung and both batters missed.

"Strike three! You're out and you're out. Let's hear it for these men, Jammy Carter and Bill Capp." He waited for the applause to die down before he said, "I know what some of you are thinking. Those boys swung wild on purpose, but that's not so. The truth is Switch Jackson is the master of precision. Would you like to see more?"

Elmo and Tommy carried out a waist high table. They set it over home plate and lined up five metal milk bottles on it like the ones you'd see in a shill game on a carny midway.

"Now, folks," Pearly gestured grandly toward the table. "You see before you five bottles, and in a demonstration of pitching prowess, Switch Jackson is going to throw five balls and knock down all five bottles, one with each pitch. And just to let you know he ain't just pitchin' and hopin', he's gonna start with the one in the middle."

Switch threw a sharp curve ball that neatly picked off the center bottle. Then with the next three pitches, toppled three more. "Now, ladies and gentlemen," Pearly said, "it gets difficult. Switch Jackson will knock down the final bottle blindfolded." Elmo ran out and as Switch stood toe to the rubber, tied a red bandanna over his eyes.

"Now, so that Switch can achieve this feat, we must have silence as I guide his pitch by sound alone. Silence, please." Pearly stood beside the table and pulled a white tipped magician's wand from his sleeve. He tapped the wand on the last bottle in a steady pinging pulse. The crowd held its breath.

Switch took his windup, and never moving his feet from their position, threw a fastball that shot straight as an arrow to the plate and knocked down the bottle. The crowd yelled and whistled.

Amos and Petey started up the baseline passing the hat. "It's worth a penny, it's worth a nickel, it's worth a dollar to see what you just saw," Pearly crowed. "Show Switch you appreciate the magic."

"I still can't see how he does that," Tommy said.

"He had his last pitch lined up and his whole body in position before Elmo put the blindfold on him," Tory replied. "All he had to do was throw the ball."

"I know that," Tommy snorted. "But what I can't see is how he makes it work."

"Like Jeff says, if you can think it, you can do it. Plus it helps there's a pinhole in the bandanna."

In the eighth inning, things heated up. Elmo got on first, ran to second when Petey hit a single, then stole third by leapfrogging over the Tornadoes' third baseman as he bent to scoop up the ball. The tide had shifted; the crowd abandoned the home team and was rooting for the Wizards.

Switch went to bat. Iron Mike's first pitch went high and inside, and if Switch hadn't thrown himself backward, it would have caught him square in the head. If it was intentional, it was a bad mistake. The catcher missed the ball and as he scrambled for it, Petey sprung like a jackrabbit from first. The rattled catcher threw the ball to second, and the instant it left his hand, Elmo dashed for home plate. Petey dove between the second basemen's legs before the ball arrived and the baseman tripped over him and dropped the ball as Elmo sprinted in for the run.

The crowd's cheers were mixed with boos for what they saw as Paterson's unsportsmanlike behavior. Jeff stood impassive. No need to protest. The crowd was doing it for him. He turned to the plate where Switch was looking for direction. "Bring Petey home."

Switch tagged the next pitch and sent it bouncing between first and second. By the time the Tornadoes had control of the ball, Switch was on first and Petey on third. Not exactly home, but on the way. Tory was next and hit a pop fly to right field. Tory was out, but Petey tagged up and beat the throw home, shaving the Tornadoes' lead to one run.

That put Bill Capp at the plate. Capp singled, but Switch was thrown out at second. As he trotted to the dugout for his glove, Switch passed Jeff, who said, "Put 'em away."

In the bottom of the eighth, Switch struck out three in a row, and the Wizards were back at bat. Ollie was first and followed Jeff's motto: *always run for second.* He hit a grounder between first and second and barely beat the ball to second base. Then Harris stepped up. The crowd began chanting, "Home Run, Home Run," and Harris pointed to a spot halfway between the right baseline and the scoreboard.

Iron Mike took his windup and shot a fast ball leaning to the outside, but just in the strike zone. Harris let it pass by and didn't move. The crowd continued its chant. Paterson's second pitch went over the center of the plate and dipped as Harris swung, catching the ball on the underside of the bat and putting it in the dirt beside the catcher for a foul ball.

The catcher signaled to Iron Mike who nodded and wound up for the third pitch. It was low and outside, but Harris stepped into it and shifted his hands to bring the bat upward to meet the ball with a solid crack. He didn't run from home plate to first right away. Instead, he pointed with the bat to the spot between the baseline and center where the ball sailed over the fence and looked as if it might land in Illinois.

As he took his lap around the bases, Harris grinned and waved to the crowd which roared as if he just swam the English Channel. Ollie danced across the plate and did a handspring as Harris rounded third. The Wizards were in the lead.

Iron Mike struck out the next two batters and found himself facing Jammy. After two balls, Jammy tagged a one-hopper to right field, he was thrown out at first, and the Tornadoes came in to bat.

Switch struck out the first batter, and when the second hit a solid line drive to left field, Elmo dove for it with a move that stretched him almost horizontal and caught the ball in the web of his glove. The next batter fell to Switch's fast ball and that left Iron Mike. The field was hushed as everyone waited to see whether Switch would pay him back in kind for the head throw.

Switch toed the rubber and idly tossed the ball an inch or two in the air a few times as he studied the strike zone. He took his stance and wound up for a right-handed pitch. The ball shot at Iron Mike straight at his hip. Iron Mike danced backward as the crowd gasped. At the last instant, the pitch curved away and the ball caught the corner of the plate. "Strike one."

The crowd laughed and whistled at Paterson's discomfiture. His clenched teeth showed above his lip. Switch took off his glove and put it on his right hand. Even at forty-five feet, he could see the anger in Paterson's eyes turning to hatred. He wound up and threw a left-hander that dipped below Paterson's bat as he swung at the ball as if it were Switch's head. "Strike two."

Switch took off his glove and dropped it at his feet. He turned to the crowd, hands in the air. "Which hand for Iron Mike?" Pearly shouted. Cries of "left" and "right" seemed all but equal then a steady chant of "Left, left, left" won out.

Switch signaled to Tory and did his windup. The pitch flew dead center

Harris stepped into it and shifted to meet the ball with a solid crack.

toward the strike zone and Iron Mike swung and he would have hit it and likely knocked it out of the park if it hadn't curved an inch past the tip of his bat halfway through his swing, too late and with too much force to check. Tory sprung from his crouch and caught the ball in his mitt, falling to the ground but never dropping the ball. "Strike three! You're out!"

Iron Mike shouted something that went unheard in the roar of the crowd and threw his bat halfway to the pitcher's mound. He stomped away like a petulant child in defeat.

"How about it, folks," shouted Pearly. "Let 'em know one more time how much you enjoyed the show." As the crowd cheered again, McClannahan sidled up beside him. "I guess you keep that fifty-dollar bill today."

Pearly took the fifty from his pocket, kissed it, and flashed his trademark grin. "George, I been betting that same bill for nigh about twenty years. The day I lose it's the day I quit."

By this time Jeff joined them. George turned to Jeff and held out his hand. "You boys played one hell of a game today, Jeff."

Jeff shook his hand and said with a grin. "So did you. We usually win by five or six runs."

As Switch headed for the bus, he saw a lean woman with skin like café-au-lait in a blue dress standing in the bus's shade. She smiled and the rest of the world disappeared for a minute as Switch ran to her and threw his arms around her, picked her up and twirled her around. He kissed her and gazed into her dark eyes.

"Delores," he said, "I didn't expect to see you 'til we got to Illinois."

"I couldn't stay away, Coley. Betty told me where you'd be this week and I couldn't wait to see you. Lester and Mabel drove me up." Switch saw Delores's sister and her husband standing at a discreet distance.

"We're gonna pack up now. Tell Lester to follow the bus back to camp. I gotta clean up. I smell like a hog."

Over her shoulder Switch saw Jeff and Pearly talking to three men in suits, two black and one white. The suits were making big broad gestures and smiling like traveling salesmen. Jeff was as still and stoic as a cigar store Indian.

"What's that all about?" said Delores.

"Looks like Jeff's negotiating. That's his big word for horse trading. We'll find out soon enough. I gotta go help load the trailer."

On the bus Jeff satisfied everyone's curiosity. "Those black gentlemen you saw me talking to are from the Negro Baseball League, Mister Hatcher and Mister Tippet . The white man is a promoter named Bridges." Jeff was careful never to use epithets like "ofay" or "cracker" when he spoke and discouraged their use by the team. "If you talk about them that way," he would say, "it makes them think they can call you whatever they want, too."

Jeff went on, "They have an all star team from the Negro League barnstorming around the Midwest and they want to play us an exhibition game in eleven days in a town called Macklin, Illinois. They're paying us two hundred dollars. Thing is, we have to play it straight, by the rules."

There was some murmuring and grumbling. Jeff put up his hand. "This ain't a show, it's a legitimate game. And it's a chance for the big boys to see what we're made of. There'll be people from all over the league there, and if they like what they see, some of you might get your chance to sign with the pros and have a real career. I'm old now, and I can't do this forever. I won't stand in the way of anybody gets a shot at a better life."

"What if they want to bring the team into the League?" Petey said.

Jeff shook his head. "I don't know what I'd do if it came to that. We'll cross that bridge if somebody builds it." His speech over, Jeff sat down and stared out the bus window at the pastures and trees.

"Man, imagine getting a job with a regular team in the League," said Petey.

"I don't know how much different it'd be," said Elmo. "The pay might be regular, but between the lean weeks and the fat ones, I don't think we'd make much more money. The owners and the managers would take the biggest chunk and we'd still be making fifty cents a day."

"What do you think, Switch? Would you jump over?"

"What? And play by the rules?" He laughed. "What fun would that be?"

Back at the camp, Switch took a bath in the creek and dressed in his good trousers and shirt. When he came out of the tent, his teammates were piling onto the bus for another run at Rockland. Switch stayed behind. Delores was waiting for him with a picnic basket and a blanket over her arm, Lester and Mabel along to chaperone.

They found a tree-shaded nook at a bend in the creek that made the spot almost an island. Switch spread the blanket and Delores unpacked the basket. Fried chicken, potato salad and greens with apple pie for dessert all sitting on a slab of ice to keep it cold along with bottles of beer.

Lester and Mabel were an odd match, he tall and lanky and she short and round as a pumpkin. Mabel had Delores's face, but spread out a little by cheeks and jowls. Lester looked as if he'd been cobbled together out of spare parts, one eye a little bit wider than the other, and a thick lower lip paired with a thin upper one. He was as quiet as she was talkative.

"Momma wants to know when you're gonna marry Delores, Coley."

"You tell your momma I will as soon as I can get a job in one place where I can make enough money to have a decent home for her to live in. I can't do that topping onions in some farmer's field for fifteen cents a day. In the meantime, I'll do what I do best 'til the damn Depression's over: throw a baseball. Besides, the road ain't no life for a woman."

"Says you," Delores jumped in. "I can cook a far sight better than Amos can."

Switch nodded. "You got me there, honey. This is the best chicken I ever tasted."

"Don't change the subject. What about this big game everybody's talking about? What if one of the leagues offered you a steady job? You'd still be on the road, but you'd be based in one city. And your pay would be regular." Delores raised an eyebrow. "What then?"

Switch laughed. "Like Jeff said, I'll cross that bridge when they build it."

"What about the team?" said Lester. "What if the league opened a slot for the Wizards? What would Jeff do?"

"I don't know if Jeff would give up the show to play straight baseball."

"Why not?"

"In his prime, Jeff was one of the best hitters and fastest base runners around. Everybody said so, but he never got the chance to prove it because just like now, baseball was a white man's game. The Negro League wasn't even established yet, so Jeff's best days came and went in pickup games where nobody even knew his name.

"The Wizards? I guess you could say that we're Jeff's testament to the white baseball establishment. When we play white teams, we win every time. But if we come at them head on, then we're uppity and the locals start grabbing for their white hoods. So we put on the show. We clown, and we do tricks, and we beat them, but it doesn't sting 'cause they're laughing all the while."

Switch downed the last swallow of his beer. He stared across the creek at the setting sun. "Jeff said once that we're like the court jester back in the days of kings and queens and such. The jester could poke fun at the king, tell him the hard truths in the form of a joke, and he wouldn't get his head chopped off like a fry chicken. The Wizards tell white baseball that black men are good enough to beat them at their own game, and we get away with it because of the show. I don't know that he'd give that up."

No one spoke a while. Shadows deepened and fireflies came out, dancing lights in the dark. Jeff's hand shot out and caught one in his palm.

He turned and offered his hand to Delores, a green glow leaking between his fingers. "Who else gonna snatch you a live emerald right out of the sky?"

Delores wrapped her hands around Switch's and said. "Nobody else I ever met. That's why I'll wait for you, Coley, as long as I have to."

"And that's why I love you so much, Delores, because you understand."

Sunday arrived, grey and chilly, and the Wizards rolled up the tent and climbed on the bus for the next town, Maitland. Pearly had gone there earlier in the week to broker a game with the Maitland Tigers, hometown heroes drafted largely from the ranks of the town's volunteer fire department. They'd play on Wednesday, and move on to Clovis, where Pearly had scheduled a rematch with the Comets, a black team that gave the Wizards a run for their money last time and were itching for another shot.

Pearly and Jeff rode ahead in the Model T, giving the team the opportunity on the bus to talk freely about what seemed to be the big chance for them all.

"If you could pick a team to play for, who would it be?" Tory said.

"I'd take the Pittsburgh Crawfords," Petey said.

"Not me, boy, I'd go with the Detroit Stars," said Elmo. "I hear they go to Mexico and Cuba over the winter and play year 'round, make some real money instead of starving all winter. How about you, Switch?"

"I don't know. Maybe the Memphis Red Sox. They have the worst pitchers in the league. They'd keep me 'til I died."

Everybody laughed at that. The talk drifted into other topics, but Switch stared out the bus window thinking about Delores and "what if."

A night on the bus and they were in Maitland where the Tigers played on a field that was little more than a pasture with some mowed grass. The ground was worse than irregular, it was just plain rough.

"How can they play ball on a field like this?" said Tanny.

"I guess they're used to it," Ollie replied.

"Hmph. They oughta spot us three runs."

The Tigers used the field as a strategy. They watched and waited for the right pitches that they could hit as grounders. The only thing you could count on when the ball bounced was that it could bounce any direction. Jeff played the fielders back. Better to have that extra time to see which way the ball would hop and hold a man on first than guess wrong up close and hope to tag him at second.

After three innings, Switch devised a strategy of his own, throwing the ball at the ceiling of the strike zone, forcing the batters to swing high for the ball, resulting in more foul tips and pop flies than base hits. Tory's mask was off as much as it was on as he chased pop up fouls. In the fourth inning, Switch fired a fast ball that the batter nipped with the top of his bat and the ball shot backward into Tory's mitt, which he'd put up in front of his face, as he put it, "in self-defense."

Running bases was a challenge as well. Jeff was grateful at the end of the day that no one turned or worse yet broke an ankle. The Wizards won and Pearly's fifty-dollar bill was safe, but it was a tired team that boarded the bus that night.

"Still got your fifty," Jeff said.

"You keep your eye on the ball, I keep my eye on the bill. That's how it works."

"Hey, Pearly," called Petey. "Don't book this place no more. Too much like work."

The Clovis Comets played a good game but lost six to three, never scoring a run past those Pearly spotted them. It started to rain in the seventh inning and the crowd thinned out, hurting the hat. Elmo pulled a groin muscle when he slipped and fell skidding in the mud into third base. He was safe, but he was hurting. Jeff wanted to put in a pinch runner for him, but Elmo stubbornly refused and triumphantly limped across home plate when Harris belted a homer two batters later.

"He's gonna feel that tomorrow," said Tory.

"Tomorrow hell," said Ollie. "He's feeling it now. I hope he can run again by the time we get to Macklin."

Driving out of Maitland, the bus stopped at an ice house where Jeff paid a penny for a block that he broke up and wrapped in a towel for Elmo to hold against his aching crotch. The rest went into a tub and the team took turns soaking their feet as the bus rolled on.

Macklin was a steel town, the sky twilight at noon from the mill smoke most days. Jeff chose to camp in Petersburg, a few miles away where, as he put it, "The air don't smell like my socks." There was a high school ball field in Petersburg, and the team could get in some practice time before Saturday.

Two nights before the All-Stars game Dobie showed up again.

The Wizards were passing around a poster Pearly had brought back from town. "They're all over the place," he said, "anywhere they could drive a nail."

Elmo held it up to the light. "The Negro League Baseball All-Stars versus the Moline Wizards. Featuring . . ." He frowned. "I don't recognize most of these names. I don't see Josh Gibson or Satchel Paige."

"You don't wanna see Josh Gibson or Satchel Paige," said Tanny. "Josh Gibson'd hit a line drive go right through your glove."

"I'm just as happy they didn't send Satchel Paige," said Cope. "We might have half a chance of winning."

"They're all good, and so are the men we're playing or they wouldn't be on the team, but at bottom they're just working men like us," said Petey. "We play hard, we'll do good."

"Yeah, but if there's scouts there for the League, they gonna like us a lot better if we win than if we lose."

Switch stood up and sauntered out of the tent.

"Hey, Switch," Tory called after him. "Where you going?"

"Out back. Amos's beans're coming back to bite me." The last daylight was shutting down and Switch was walking from the tent to the latrine they'd dug across the pasture when he heard a sharp whisper: "Coley."

The twilight was dim, but not so dim that Switch couldn't make out Dobie's swollen eye and his split lip. "I need help."

"I see that. Thought you were in Cleveland."

"Never mind that, man, I'm in trouble."

"Dobie, You been in trouble since the day you started to walk."

"I need money. A lot of money."

Switch snorted. "And you think I got it? If I had a lot of money, I wouldn't be ridin' in a bus, sleepin' in a tent, and shittin' in the woods."

"Look, man, they gonna kill me."

"Who's gonna kill you?"

"Mose Crabtree's men."

"Mose Crabtree, the bookie from Moline?"

Dobie nodded, a rapid jerking motion. "He's gonna kill me if I don't pay up."

"How much you owe him?"

"Two thousand dollars."

"You're a fool for putting yourself on the hook like that, and you're a bigger fool for coming to me for money. I ain't got but seven dollars in my pocket. And I sure as hell ain't giving it to you to give to some bookie."

"I know you ain't got the money to bail me out, but there's something else."

Switch's head cocked back and he looked at Dobie from the bottoms of his eyes. "Something else?"

"That game with the All-Stars this weekend. It's big news back home, a lot of people are betting on the Wizards. If you was to lose . . ."

"You want me to throw the game? Is that what you want?" Switch's voice was rising with anger.

The words tumbled out in clumps. "You don't have to lose by much. Just shave a run or two. That's all. They're the All-Stars, Coley. The Wizards lose, ain't no shame in it. Hell, you'll probably lose anyway. And I can lay some bets down for you on the side, make you some cash."

Switch's fist caught Dobie square on his chin and knocked him flat on his back.

"You think I'd sell out my team for the likes of you, you're crazy. Tell you what, Dobie, you like to gamble, you go bluff Mose, tell him I said yes, and maybe we will lose the game and you'll win. But if we lose, it's gonna be clean and honest. I ain't throwing a game for Mose, for you, for anybody. Besides, I do this one time, it won't be the last. Them dogs'll have their teeth in me forever."

Dobie started to stand, and Switch said, "You get up in my reach, I'll knock your ass down again."

Dobie scuttled backward, whining like a child. "They gonna kill me, Coley. I'm your brother. You don't care about nobody but your own self. You promised Mama…"

"Don't you even say her name. I promised her I'd take care of you, but you made a promise too; no more dice, no more cards, no more ponies. You make me sick. Get away, Dobie, and don't come back. The Wizards hear you talking, Mose won't have to kill you, they'll do it for him."

Dobie got to his feet and started for the road, his head down.

Switch walked the other direction into the darkness. As he passed a thick elm tree, he didn't see Jeff standing beside it.

Switch lay awake that night in his cot. He listened to the snores of the other players in the tent mixed with the crickets outside. Sure, he could make the Wizards lose, it would be easy to do, but Cope was right; the scouts wouldn't hire losers. This was the chance they all needed to crack the League and to prove they weren't just a gang of clowns.

Should he tell Jeff? Should he tell the team? If he did, would some of them drop a ball, throw wild to home plate, or strike out on purpose, knowing it might keep his brother alive? They'd be doing it for him, but he couldn't stand the thought they'd all be throwing their futures away because he was their friend. And if he told Jeff or anyone and they lost the game anyway, there would always be that suspicion that he gave in and lost

Switch's fist caught Dobie square on his chin...

it for them on purpose. Mama had always told him, "Be true to yourself, son; that's what makes you a man."

He decided that moment he wouldn't let the team lose. But as he rolled over and shut his eyes he knew he'd be agonizing over the decision and making it again every minute until the game was over.

The night before the game, as an extra perk Bridges arranged rooms for the team in the Royal Hotel. The team was happy about sleeping in real beds until they found out they weren't alone. The budbugs started biting as soon as the lights went out.

Just before midnight, Jeff came down the hall knocking on the doors. "Grab your gear and head for the bus. We ain't staying here 'cause we ain't sleeping."

"You think Bridges knew about the livestock?" Ollie said, climbing on the bus.

"What do you think?" Cope grumbled. "I didn't see no All-Stars hanging around the lobby."

"Well, we ain't falling for that trick," said Jeff. The loss of sleep was bad enough, but the itching of bug bites would have been a maddening distraction. "Amos, take us to the ball field. We're sleeping under the stars tonight. Praise the Lord it ain't raining."

Jeff kicked them all awake early. "Rise and shine. We're going to breakfast."

The night at the Royal included breakfast, and Jeff wasn't about to let a paid meal slide past. "And if anybody so much as says the word 'bedbug,' I'll knock you out."

Halfway through the meal, Bridges showed up, all grins and glad handing. "So, how were your rooms?"

"Slept like a baby," Jeff said with a grin. "That's the joy of a clear conscience."

Bridges' grin slipped a little but he let it pass. "Well, I'll see you fellows at the field."

The American Legion Community Baseball Field was a regulation field with a backstop, dugouts, and a four foot wire mesh fence along the sidelines fronting bleachers as far as the bases. A six-foot plank fence curved around the outfield and at its center a scoreboard stood under a trio of flagpoles, Old Glory, the Illinois state flag and the banner of the American Legion. The dew wet grass was deep green and clipped like a carpet, newly limed baselines as white as a fresh laundered shirt.

Jeff and Pearly stood at home plate and surveyed the field. Pearly grinned. "Sure ain't Maitland."

Jeff looked around the infield. "Hell ain't Maitland."

Bridges and his crew roped off the area around the field and set up ticket booths on three sides. A quarter for the bleachers and a nickel to stand or sit on the ground. Bridges chose the field well. There wasn't a hill or a tall building for a quarter mile in any direction where a body could see the game for free.

"I still don't see what it would hurt for us to put out our chairs," Pearly said.

"It's their game and they're paying us a lot more than we usually pull down," Jeff said. "Don't be greedy."

The All Stars' bus rolled in just before noon. It was shiny and new, and parked beside the Wizards' bus, it looked like Cleopatra's barge. "All Stars" swept down the side of the blue bus in white script trailed by a cluster like the Milky Way. Jeff and Pearly watched as the team filed off the bus led by manager Cobb Sims.

"There's Bobby Martin," said Jeff. "And Toby Willow—good shortstop. And look at that." Jeff pointed to a tall man as dark as a skillet. "Hey, Poxy." The big man turned and his face split into a grin. "Little Jeff." He sauntered over and eyed Jeff up and down. "You still ain't growed up after all these years."

"And you still look like some woman's husband come after you with a .410." Poxy's nickname came from the smallpox scars that cratered his face but were lost in his color five feet away.

"Me and Jeff used to play on different teams against each other back when he didn't have wrinkles in his face like an old shoe," Poxy explained to Pearly. "I hear you're the manager of this bunch."

Jeff nodded. "Yep. That's me. What're you? Bat boy?"

Poxy laughed and Pearly realized this sniping banter was a ritual between old rivals. "I'm the batting and base line coach. What do you think about that?"

"I think the All-Stars are doomed."

Poxy cackled and slapped his thigh. "I could outgun Jeff on the diamond one day or the other, but nobody could ever get past him at the dozens." He slapped Jeff on the shoulder. "Good to see you, Jeff. I'm looking forward to the game. Just like old times." He trotted off after the team who was headed for their dugout.

By the time the warm-ups were over, the bleacher seats were filled and people stood two and three deep along the fences. Vendors with trays hanging on neck straps hawked peanuts, popcorn and hot dogs to a crowd that skipped lunch for a good spot at the fence.

Switch stood beside Jeff and watched the All-Stars' batting practice. "That one, Cooper," said Jeff nodding toward a stocky batter leaning into the plate. "He drops his shoulder when he swings, like an uppercut. Him you can play like a banjo." Jeff had been coaching Switch for the last fifteen minutes, pointing out strengths and weaknesses in the batters. Switch took out the baseballs he always carried, one in each pocket and squeezed them in his hands.

"You want I should pitch left or right?"

"You're a big boy; you decide. Whichever arm feels best."

Poxy came over and stood between Jeff's line of sight and the plate. "Hey, Jeff, is this the famous Switch Jackson I heard so much about?" Then to Switch, "Where'd you get that fancy glove?" He pointed to Clarice hanging by the back strap from Switch's belt.

"Go away, Poxy," Jeff snorted. I'm working." He stepped to the side to see the plate and Poxy laughed. "Same old Jeff. All work and no play."

"I guess for us play is work," said Switch stepping to the other side of Poxy, who laughed again and walked away.

"You handled him right," said Jeff. "That man plays half of his game in your head. Distraction's a major tactic."

Just before the start of the game, two rows of the right field bleachers that had been roped off filled up with men in suits. Switch recognized Bridges, Hatcher and Tippet among them. "There's the nabobs."

Jeff scanned the dignitaries. "They're all from the League. Give 'em an eyeful."

The All-Stars had the home-team advantage and took the field first. An American Legion Honor Guard marched onto the field with flags and rifles followed by the Macklin High School Marching Band who struck up "The Star Spangled Banner." Jim Wheaton, the home plate umpire shouted, "Play Ball!" and the crowd roared like a waterfall.

In the dugout, Jeff called the team around him. "No showboating. Keep it simple. Put on your Sunday best and show these people we ain't just a bunch of clowns."

"When's the last time we played for a crowd this big?" said Cope, tightening his shoelaces.

"Can't say as I remember," said Tanny.

"Fifty people or fifty thousand makes no difference," said Jeff. "Only ones count's the ones on the field. Just get your ass out there and play the game."

The All-Stars were pitching Wash Pickens, a lefty from the Monarchs, famous for his fast ball, who delivered in the first inning, striking out two and scooping up Petey's bunt to make a double play.

Switch took the mound and allowed himself one look around the crowd. Though he couldn't see her, he knew Delores was one of the faces in that mob of people, and he hoped that Dobie wasn't, that he had enough sense to run for his life. He looked to Jeff who was standing in his usual position along the third base line where he could see and be seen by everyone.

The first All Star batter was Tommy Petrie, a fielder from the Crawfords. Switch put him down with three straight strikes and the crowd cheered. They weren't partial. After striking out another man, Switch threw an outsider that the batter nipped into a pop fly that Tory pulled in with ease. Three up, three down.

The next three innings were scoreless. The teams were both playing hard and playing good. The hits were solid, but the fielding was extraordinary. The crowd caught the fever and cheered for performance regardless of the team.

In the fifth inning, Harris tagged a pitch that sent a line drive bouncing off the left field wall for a double that drove Elmo home for the first run of the game. Wash struck out the next two and retired the side, but blood was drawn, the All-Stars had yet to get a man on base, and the game could only become more intense.

Wash struck out Tory and Cope after him, then it was Switch's turn at bat. He'd watched Wash with a pitcher's eye for five innings now and also with a gambler's eye for tells. Most people couldn't see at forty-five what Switch could. Every time Wash threw a curve ball, the tip of his tongue showed at the corner of his mouth. Every time he threw a slider, his right eye opened just a tad wider than his left.

He'd told Jeff what he observed but Jeff said he couldn't do much with the information. "By the time I could signal the batter, the ball would be on its way. Besides, I don't want them looking at me; I want them watching the pitch. Tell the others if you want, but I don't know how many of them have your eyes."

Switch stepped into the batter's box and took his left-handed stance. He watched Wash closely, waiting to see if he would give away his pitch. Wash's eyebrow lifted and as expected, he threw a slider that flew just outside the zone. "Ball."

On the next pitch, Wash's tongue showed between his lips and when the curve ball came, Switch was ready. His swing connected and the ball hopped between first and second into the outfield. It was picked up by the center fielder too quickly for a double, so Switch had to content himself with first base.

Ollie was up next with Cap Miller on deck. Ollie hit a fly ball to center field. Switch tagged up when Petrie caught the ball, but the All-Stars were just too quick. He'd've been thrown out at second for sure, so he stayed at first, leading off base with every pitch.

Cap tried a bunt that rolled to the mound. Moving faster than a human ought to, Wash sprinted for it, scooped it up and in a spinning move turned and fired it to second for the force out. Cap ran fast, but the ball was faster. Double play.

Switch stayed in the field and Elmo brought Clarice as he ran to center. He threw the glove to Switch and gave him a thumbs-up. Nobody dared jinx him by wishing him luck or saying the words "no hitter," but the possibility hung in the air. The All-Stars tagged a few of his pitches the sixth inning, but the Wizard fielders earned their keep and held the opposition at zero.

Tanny got on base and Harris was up. Jeff saw Wash look to the dugout, hesitate a moment, then nod his head. Four straight pitches went low and outside, walking the biggest threat in the Wizards' lineup. The crowd booed, but Wash ignored them. He struck out Petey and Tory, retiring the side, leaving two men on and the score at one-nothing.

During the seventh-inning stretch the band did a creditable job of "The Stars and Stripes Forever". While they played, Switch spotted Delores waving to him from the crowd along the right field fence. He waved back, and then the song ended and he was back on the mound.

The first batter was the top of the All-Stars' lineup, B. B. Waters from the Homestead Grays, a power hitter. He entered the batter's box as the umpire brushed dirt from the plate. Waters showed his teeth to Switch, but it was no friendly grin. As he took his stance, Waters put his left foot forward, cocking back his right hip.

Switch fired a fastball that dropped just as Waters' bat crossed the plate. It thumped into Tory's mitt for a strike. On the second pitch, Waters hunched slightly to catch the ball head on and send it parallel to the ground in a blistering line drive up the center that would have taken Switch's head off if he hadn't caught it in Clarice's webbing. Waters cursed and flung the bat, earning him a rebuke and a warning from the umpire.

Next up was Tommy Shelton from the Claybrook Tigers. Shelton crouched in, crowding the plate for the first two pitches, both of which barely caught the outside corner of the plate. When Switch fired the third,

Shelton threw himself backward as if to avoid the ball and twisted his right hip into the pitch.

The Wizards all braced themselves to run in and defend Switch if the All-Stars swarmed out of the dugout, but they didn't move. Jeff and Cobb conferred with Wheaton at the plate. There were some raised voices and flapping arms. Wheaton called a hit batter, and Shelton trotted to first base. Switch got a warning.

The crowd booed, but Switch understood they weren't booing him; they were booing Cobb's underhanded tactics. Get a man on first however you have to, rattle the pitcher, then bat the cleanup man to drive in a run and tie the game, or better yet, hit a homer and take the lead. And now Switch was warned. If he hit another batter, he'd be out of the game with nobody nearly as good to take his place.

The cleanup batter was Ted Whitson. He wasn't Josh Gibson, but he could hit a long ball. Switch looked to Jeff to see whether he'd signal him to walk the batter. Jeff didn't move an eyebrow. The message was clear: don't play like they play.

Whitson knocked the first two pitches foul but both went over the fence, long hits that were close enough to homers to make the Wizards nervous. Tory signaled for a curve and repeated the signal. Switch saw Whitson's eyes twitch toward the first base line. Switch threw a drop ball, signaled by Tory's coded repetition. Whitson swung for the curve and his bat swished through empty space as the ball slammed into Tory's mitt. Strike three.

Some spotter on the sideline was reading Tory's signals and warning the batters. It was all on Switch now. He hoped Tory was ready for some surprises.

Tory continued to signal Switch, signals he ignored as he struck out the third batter who looked more befuddled by each pitch. The All Stars weren't fools. They'd know Switch was onto them, but it felt so good to dust them off in front of the crowd.

In the eighth inning, the All-Stars tried another trick. Poxy strolled out to Jeff's vantage point along the third base line and blocked his view of the field. Jeff said something to him no one could hear and Poxy laughed at him and patted him on the head like a little boy. Jeff said another something to Poxy and raised his shirt an inch. The big man's eyes grew wide and he backed away as if Jeff had turned into a rattlesnake.

The eighth inning became what the Pittsburgh Pirates' broadcast announcer Rosey Rowswell called a "pitcher's duel." Benny Torrance walked to first, but neither team got so much as one base hit.

At the top of the ninth Wash's fast ball scorched a hole through the strike zone and sent Tanny and Cap back to the bench, leaving Elmo to face him. After a strike and a ball, Elmo caught a sinker that went hopping through the infield and he took off for first base. Halfway up the baseline, he suddenly pitched forward, clutching at the inside of his thigh. His groin injury had come back to haunt him. To his credit, Elmo staggered on in spite of the pain, but an easy throw to first retired the side.

Jeff sent in Billy Potts to cover center field. "Now's your chance, son," Jeff said. Make us proud."

The crowd began chanting "no hit, no hit" and the pressure was on. The bottom of the ninth lineup was Willow, Waters, and Shelton, then Whitson, the All-Stars' hit machine. Switch was about to pitch his first ball to Willow when he heard a plaintive "Coley!" from the crowd. He looked past Jeff and saw beyond him three men in suits shoving their way through the crowd to the left field fence.

Dobie was flanked by a pair of thugs, one a big man in a blue suit and a fedora and the other a tawny little devil in a burgundy suit and a white panama hat. They had Dobie by the arms against the fence. "Coley!" Dobie yelled again over the chanting crowd. Jeff looked over his shoulder then turned his gaze back to Switch. Jeff said nothing and did nothing but fix Switch with his stare.

Switch delivered a curve that whistled past Waters for a strike. The crowd roared. His second pitch was low and outside for a ball. Waters swung and missed an inside curve, and the crowd began chanting "Switch, Switch, Switch." He forced himself to not look at Dobie and sent a blazing four finger fast ball past Waters for the third strike.

Shelton took his stance and crowded the plate again. He silently mouthed the words "hit me" and unwrapped the middle finger of his left hand from the bat for a quick obscene gesture. Switch threw to the outside and Shelton checked his swing in time for a ball. Switch threw a slider that caught the outside corner of the plate for a strike and the crowd picked up the "no hit" chant again. Shelton shifted his feet and Switch realized that this was the pitch Shelton would step into.

The strategy was simple: aim where the bat will be.

Switch threw a two finger fast ball and as he expected, Shelton twisted his torso back while thrusting his hip into the strike zone. But this time, Shelton brought the bat around in a checked swing to make it look good. The ball caromed off the bat and flew into the stands for a foul ball. "Strike two."

The crowd went crazy. The chant of "no hit" became an indefinable roar. Shelton couldn't try his trick again. Switch threw a four-finger fast ball, but Shelton got lucky. The ball struck the trademark and the bat broke in two, sending a grounder up the third base line. The ball hopped in not out, and Shelton was a second too quick for the throw.

The crowd groaned. The no-hitter was over. Shelton was on base, and Ted Whitson was up. Things got quiet in a hurry. Switch threw a hard curve that made Whitson check his swing but it sailed into Tory's mitt for a strike. A second fast ball slid past Whitson's bat.

Against his better judgment, Switch glanced toward Delores and as he turned back to the plate his eye caught a flash of reflection from his right. The man in the maroon suit was holding a knife so that the blade flashed in the sun. When he saw Switch was watching, he put it to Dobie's throat, shielding it from the crowd around him with his white hat.

Switch decided for the last time. He took off his glove and set it on the mound beside him. Cobb was out of the dugout in a heartbeat, pointing at Switch and shouting at Wheaton. "What's he up to? He's gonna pull some stunt."

Wheaton looked to Switch and back to Cobb. "Show me a rule in the book that says any player has to wear a glove. Get off the field."

Cobb stormed back to the dugout. The crowd didn't breathe. Switch looked to Delores and kissed the ball. He didn't look at Dobie. Whitson bared his teeth.

Switch wound up and let fly. He threw a three-finger changeup calculated to throw off Whitson's timing.

It worked.

Whitson swung and missed, but Switch didn't see any of it. The second the pitch left the mound, he thrust a hand in each pocket. He pivoted to the third base line and with each hand fired a fast ball at the fence. The one from his right caught the big gangster square in the forehead. The one from his left caught the knife man on the bridge of his nose.

As soon as the balls left his hands, Switch sprinted for the dugout where he grabbed a bat and vaulted the fence. The crowd jumped back, unsure of what was happening. The knife man was pushing himself up with one hand, his blade in the other when Switch brought the bat down on his shoulder, shattering the assassin's collarbone making his knife arm useless. The big man rushed Switch and Switch connected with his head making a sound like an ax in a stump.

As the big man fell, Switch saw Mose Crabtree behind him pulling a pistol from beneath his vest. As the gun went off, Dobie jumped at Switch, hoping to push him out of the bullet's path and stepping into it himself.

As Dobie fell, Mose aimed the pistol at Switch's head.

A second shot.

Mose clutched at his chest and stared at the spreading red stain on his white shirt front. On the other side of the fence, Jeff held his pistol with both hands, smoke lazily looping from the muzzle.

Switch knelt, cradling Dobie's head in the crook of his arm. Dobie looked up at Switch and smiled. "You come through for me, big brother. I knew you would."

"And you come through for me too," Switch said.

"I'll tell Mama when I see her you kept your promise." His eyes drifted upward to the sky. "It's beautiful over there. Beautiful." His eyes closed in death. Delores knelt beside Switch and wrapped arms of comfort around his shoulders, crying his tears.

Then Tory pushed through the crowd holding Clarice. He held the glove out to Switch. "You left this on the mound."

Switch raised his hand to take it, hesitated, and took Delores's hand instead. He shook his head. "Ain't gonna need it no more. I'm going home."

The End

The Negro Baseball League

When I was ten years old, I had the privilege of watching the Pittsburgh Pirates play the New York Yankees at Forbes Field, so my appreciation of baseball has deep roots. When Ron mentioned that he needed a baseball story for an anthology, my first inclination was to write about the Negro Baseball league since it has such an interesting history full of unique characters. The further I thought about the story the more I leaned toward a barnstorming show team. The Negro Baseball League featured one team that included comedy in its play, but I wanted the Moline Wizards to be, as Pearly Stubbs says, "more like a rodeo," winning not just the game but the crowd and proving to the white baseball establishment that black players were as good or better while using the court jester role to tell a hard truth to a society not yet ready to hear it.

●●●

FRED ADAMS JR. - is a lifelong fan of pulp fiction who has been writing and publishing genre fiction since 1971. He is the creator of the *Hitwolf* series, the *C. O. Jones* series, and the *Six Gun Terrors* series for Airship 27 Productions and has contributed stories to a number of Airship anthologies. Fred recently retired from his position as an English Professor for Penn State University and lives in Mount Pleasant, Pennsylvania where he "gets up every morning and writes" and still plays guitar solo and with bands in local venues.

UNCLE BOB'S BROWNING

(A Personal Memoir)

by
Richard L. Kellogg

Growing up on a small dairy farm in western New York, it is not surprising that the rod and the gun were constant companions during my formative years. Whether casting for trout along the shady banks of a stream or stalking pheasants in apple orchards, there was a sense of mystery and adventure about outdoor pursuits which has persisted to this day.

I hunted and fished with my father when he could escape for a few hours from the pressures of his work on the farm. However, my favorite comrade for such activities was my Uncle Bob. Aunt Gladys and Uncle Bob lived in a suburb of Buffalo, New York, where my uncle was employed at a steel foundry. A childless couple, they frequently spent weekends relaxing at my parent's farm. During these visits, I delighted in wandering along the streams and exploring the deep woods with my uncle.

As a young boy, I was awed with my uncle's affluence and the vast sums that he spent on his hobbies. My father, for example, used a battered single-shot gun when hunting deer. Uncle Bob sported a fancy Browning pump-action shotgun in the field. I managed with an old bamboo fishing pole while Uncle Bob transported expensive casting rods in the trunk of his shiny Buick Roadmaster. I thought that my uncle must be an extremely wealthy man. I didn't realize until later years that he actually worked at a rather dirty and dangerous job in a factory.

To his credit, Uncle Bob was a sportsman in the best sense of the word. He taught me how to handle firearms safely and the importance of obeying all the hunting and fishing regulations. The safety catch must stay on until you are ready to fire. Always unload the weapon before crossing fences. Do not carry a loaded gun near the highway or in the vicinity of buildings. Never point the gun at anything you do not intend to shoot. Perhaps most important, guns and alcohol are a dangerous mixture and must not be used together. These were all crucial lessons and he taught them well.

A troubling situation involving my Uncle Bob started to unfold during deer season in November many years ago. Prior to this puzzling event, I thought-at the ripe old age of twelve- that I understood the world and the people in it fairly well. Most events in my life made sense and I assumed they always would. Human behavior was seen as safe, predictable, logical, and often boring. At least, this was my view of the universe prior to the strange hunting episode.

Uncle Bob and Aunt Gladys arrived at our home on Friday evening to begin a week's vacation in the country. My mother and Aunt Gladys planned to spend their time visiting, shopping, and preparing for the Thanksgiving feast which was scheduled for the following week. Uncle Bob relished outside activities such as chopping wood for the kitchen stove and helping to feed and care for the livestock. Most important to me, my uncle had promised me that I could accompany him on a deer hunt. Although I was too young to purchase a hunting license, he assured me that I could provide an extra set of eyes to watch for the game. I also had a strong back which would help haul the trophy buck from the woods back to the farm.

"How you doing, Skipper? Ready for the big hunt?" Uncle Bob yelled as I ran out to help unload the Buick. Aunt Gladys gave me a big hug and we proceeded to move suitcases and clothing from the car to the house.

As the adults sat around the living room drinking coffee and chatting of activities planned for the following week, I sat over in the corner and visualized my first deer hunt. Since my eyes were younger and sharper than my uncle, I would spot the large buck skulking through the brush before he did. My uncle was an excellent marksman and, with only one shot, the deer would fall over dead right on the spot. We would then, working together, drag the animal several miles through the snow and receive a hero's welcome at home. My parents would record the historic event with their Kodak. We would all dine on delicious venison for the remainder of the winter.

Someone slapped me on the back. "Wake up, kid. It's time for bed. You need your rest for the big hunt." I looked up at a laughing Uncle Bob and felt sheepish. Falling asleep in front of adults was childish. However, it had been a long day and I was more than ready for bed.

That weekend seemed to drag on forever. Saturday morning, my mother and Aunt Gladys went shopping in the nearby village and stocked up on groceries. My dad was having a problem with leaky water buckets in the barn so my uncle and I were drafted for plumbing duties. By afternoon, the cows could drink once again without water dripping down onto their grain.

Sunday was the ordained day for all of us to attend religious services at the First Baptist Church in the village. This was followed by a delightful turkey dinner and good conversation around the dining room table of the old farmhouse.

That evening, Uncle Bob assembled all his hunting gear in preparation for the opening day of deer season. All of his clothing was bright red – his cap, vest, coat, trousers, socks, and gloves. As I recall, he carried matches, a compass, a knife, a rope, and shotgun shells in his coat pockets. There was a large pocket in the back of his coat for holding sandwiches, apples, cookies, and a thermos of coffee. My uncle was a short, stocky man and always carried enough food for two ordinary men. He instructed me in cleaning and oiling the action of his Browning so that it would be in prime shape for the critical moment of the hunt. He pumped the shotgun several times and proclaimed that I had done a commendable job.

I slept only fitfully that night. I dreamt of pursuing a majestic eight-point buck deer. But the deer was not in the woods where it rightfully belonged. Instead, it was hiding in our herd of Holstein dairy cows, which was grazing in our lower pasture. In the honored tradition of Gene Autry and Roy Rogers, I was attempting to rope the deer with a lariat. No matter how fast I ran, the deer would run faster and dart back and forth within the group of cows. Invariably, the rope would fly through the air toward the buck but drop down around the head of one of the cows. I am not sure what significance Dr. Freud would have attached to this particular dream but it was vivid and somewhat unsettling. Segments of the cow-roping dream ran through my mind for several days.

Monday morning, as predicted by the weatherman on the radio, blossomed sunny and cold. There were several inches of fresh snow on the ground and temperatures would hover just below freezing for most of the day. It seemed the ideal day for my first day of hunting with Uncle Bob.

I awoke to the sound of voices from the downstairs kitchen. The door at the foot of the stairs opened with a bang. My uncle shouted, "Let's go, Skip. The deer are waiting. Today's the day!"

"Coming, coming," I replied, and stumbled out of my warm bed onto the cold floor, shivering both from cold and excitement. I dressed quickly in the dark and hurried downstairs.

Dad had already gone to the barn to begin his morning chores of feeding and milking the cows. Mercifully, I had been excused from my usual farm duties for the day. Aunt Gladys, Uncle Bob, and my mother were drinking coffee and finishing up a plate of pancakes and sausages when I arrived.

My aunt passed the plate of pancakes in my direction and my mother poured me a cup of steaming coffee. "Your mother and I," said Aunt Gladys, "have been sharing our recipes for venison. We need that meat to get us through the winter. You and Bob had better not let us down."

Mother sipped her coffee and smiled. "Gladys, we have enough beef, chicken, and pork here on the farm to survive. However, the venison can be our dessert."

My uncle, already dressed in bright red and looking like a mischievous Santa Claus, laughed loudly and leaned back in his chair. "You can count on Skipper and me," he boasted. "We know every inch of that wood lot and the location of every deer trail. With any luck, we will be home with a nice buck by noon."

Before we left, my aunt told Uncle Bob not to get too tired and not to wander too far from the farmhouse. He just smiled and told her she shouldn't fret. He was feeling fine.

Uncle Bob was certainly in a good mood that morning and I looked forward to spending the day in his company. He had shot three deer on our farm in previous years so I was optimistic he would be successful again. Although he was overweight and, according to Aunt Gladys, smoked too much, his outdoor activities kept him active and in fairly good health.

In our earlier strategy meeting around the breakfast table, it was decided that we would hunt in the large wooded area north of the house and barn. This section adjoined our hayfield and contained adequate brush and new growth of timber to support a thriving deer population. Uncle Bob had hunted this region many times for small game and frequently bagged his limit of rabbits and squirrels.

Everything seemed normal the first few hours of the hunt. We located a large log on a hillside, which overlooked a fairly open valley. Uncle Bob and I brushed off the snow and sat on the log to wait for the deer to pass below us. It appeared to be the ideal location and we hadn't seen any other hunters on our hike back into the woods. I noticed that my uncle looked rather pale. He was perspiring and breathing heavily by the time we reached our destination.

We had waited patiently and quietly for nearly an hour when things began to go terribly wrong. Uncle Bob touched me on the shoulder and whispered, "Quiet, Skipper. Here comes a deer."

I turned my head slowly to the left and to the right but could not see a deer to save my life. In fact, it was almost eerily quiet except for a light breeze rustling the tree branches above us. Like the dog in the nighttime,

"Quiet, Skipper. Here comes a deer."

even the birds and the chipmunks were noticeable for their absence.

"I don't see anything. Where is it?" I whispered back. I glanced over at my uncle and saw that his hands were shaking. A film of sweat could be seen on his forehead and above his lips. He was mumbling to himself and staring, a glazed look in his eyes, at a large pile of brush about fifty yards down the hill to his right.

Uncle Bob pulled up his Browning shotgun and pointed it in the general direction of the brush pile. My uncle prided himself on being a steady shot but the barrel wavered back and forth. I continued to scan the whole area around the brush pile but didn't see any movement at all.

"I see that sucker now," exclaimed my uncle. He snapped off the safety, aimed the gun, and fired. The unexpected roar of the twelve-gauge startled me and I nearly fell backwards off the log. Bob leaped up from the log and pumped his shotgun to prepare for a second shot.

Suddenly, much to my amazement, a red-garbed hunter stepped out from behind a tree near the brush pile. At the top of his voice, he began screaming, "You crazy fools! What in the devil is wrong with you? Your bullet missed me by only a few feet!" He was a large, angry man and he moved toward us with fire in his eyes.

Uncle Bob blinked several times, stepped back, and handed me his shotgun. He looked like he was about to burst into tears. Within a few seconds, my uncle was quickly transformed into an old and very frightened man.

"I am terribly sorry," he pleaded to the stranger. "Nothing like this has ever happened to me before. I thought there was a deer moving behind the brush pile. Please forgive me."

My uncle began to cry. He rubbed his nose and eyes with the sleeve of his hunting coat. All the color left his face and his lips were trembling. He could not speak.

The rage began to fade from the eyes of the other hunter. This total stranger, whom I did not recognize and would never see again, must have sensed that my uncle was falling apart before his very eyes. He approached my uncle and gently placed an arm around his shoulder. With a compassion that is still hard for me to fathom, the hunter said softly, "It's alright. It's alright. You just made a mistake. You and your partner better call it a day. We don't need any more close calls."

The hunter asked me if I could handle things by myself. I assured him that I could, thanked him, and shook his hand before he disappeared into the woods. I told my uncle that I was scared and that we had better start walking home. My appetite for hunting deer had vanished. Uncle Bob looked around, shook his head, and looked totally bewildered. "Home. Home. Where is home?" he asked. "I do not remember where home is." He acted as if he were frightened and about to start weeping again.

I attempted to feign a confidence, which I did not really feel. "Don't worry, Uncle Bob. You have had a bad experience. I know the way back to the farm," I reassured him. "We have plenty of time to get home before it gets dark."

Upon my request, my uncle meekly allowed me to unload his Browning and carry it on the way home. After walking for nearly an hour, we halted under a pine tree to eat our sandwiches and apples. I can't recall ever having such a mournful lunch. We were both shivering from the cold and neither spoke a word during the entire meal. Uncle Bob stared off into space and I tried to think of reasons to explain my uncle's strange behavior. The whole world seemed to go askew that afternoon.

Unfortunately, despite my bravado, I had only been in the woods a few times and did not know the way home. With me in the lead, we wandered around the woods all afternoon. As lost people often do, we were probably traveling in a circle. No other hunters crossed our path that unhappy day. Late in the afternoon, a large buck came crashing through the trees within firing range. We ignored it completely.

Uncle Bob didn't say much as we struggled to find a way out of the forest. Several times, he mumbled that "Gladys will be upset. Gladys will be upset." This thought seemed to bother him more than the fact that he had nearly killed another human being. It was a mystery to me as to why my uncle, a skilled and experienced outdoorsman, would shoot wildly into a brush pile. Stranger yet, how could he possibly get lost in an area where he had hunted for many years? These questions made my head spin and I was unable to come up with any reasonable solutions.

As dusk was approaching, I was becoming colder and colder. It looked like we would have to spend the night in the woods and this prospect was far from appealing. I speculated on the safest way and place to start a fire. I wondered whether we could gather enough dry branches to keep a fire going throughout the long winter night. I hoped that my parents would be out searching for us by now.

As I was musing about our unhappy situation, Uncle Bob suddenly laughed and gave me a hard poke in the ribs. "Look, Skipper," he exclaimed, "I see a light through the trees. It must be the farmhouse." He took the gun from me and, regaining command for the moment, pointed into the trees.

Bobbing my head up and down, I could also see a light twinkling in the distance. Civilization was once again within our grasp. The nightmare was nearly over.

When we tramped out of the woods toward the highway, my heart sank for a moment. The building in front of us was not the familiar and welcoming farmhouse from which we had departed in the morning. This little ranch house belonged to the Johnson's, neighbors who lived nearly two miles from my parent's house. I went to the door and quickly explained our plight to Mrs. Johnson. Her main reaction to our being lost was the statement that, "It happens to the best of us." She invited us in to telephone my parents for a ride home. It was wonderful to be warm and comfortable again. Maybe things would turn out all right after all.

Within a few minutes, the Roadmaster came purring up to the front porch with Aunt Gladys at the wheel. My aunt and my parents looked very worried and didn't stay long. They thanked Mrs. Johnson for her kindness, loaded Uncle Bob and me into the backseat, and headed the car for home.

My parents probably realized that something was wrong but they didn't ask many questions. I told them that we had gotten lost in the woods but did not mention that Uncle Bob had accidentally fired his gun in the direction of another hunter. My uncle also chose not to comment on that painful event. He spoke very little the rest of the evening and went to bed early.

When I got up the following morning, my aunt and uncle were eating breakfast with my parents. Their suitcases were already packed and sitting by the door. Everyone looked tired and there was a feeling of sadness in the room.

Aunt Gladys cleared her throat and told me that Uncle Bob was not feeling at all well. Getting lost in the woods had quite exhausted him. She concluded by saying, "Bob needs to see his doctor for an examination so we are leaving early. We will plan to spend Thanksgiving together next year."

I responded that it was a good hunt, even though we did get lost for a while. "We'll get that deer when Uncle Bob feels better."

Uncle Bob joined in, "You bet your life, Skipper. You are the best hunting buddy a man could have. I'd still be up in the woods except for you."

After their departure, my parents and I stood on the front porch and watched the red Buick fade into the distance down the highway. I still wondered about my uncle's behavior and whether he would get well enough to go hunting again.

Aunt Gladys phoned my mother a few days after Thanksgiving and inquired about how we had spent the holiday. She said that a team of doctors had evaluated Uncle Bob and that the report was not good. The physicians were fairly certain that my uncle was experiencing a severe and sudden onset of Alzheimer's disease. Apparently his confusion and disorientation during our hunt were symptoms reflecting a serious problem with the nerve cells of his brain.

Although the bizarre behavior of Uncle Bob on the hunting trip was now more understandable, not a great deal could be done to remedy the problem. My uncle soon retired from his job and lived only two more years after the onset of his illness. He could not travel anywhere by himself since he could not find his way back home. He became unusually withdrawn and could not recognize friends and relatives he had known for years. Aunt Gladys brought Uncle Bob out to visit the farm several times before his death. However, he rarely spoke. He would nod his head agreeably and smile when we talked to him. I would like to believe that he recognized me but maybe that is only wishful thinking.

Although we never went deer hunting again, Uncle Bob left me his Browning shotgun. We still pursue that elusive buck in the world of dreams. And we never get lost.

The End

RICHARD L. KELLOGG - lives in upstate New York and is a Professor Emeritus of Psychology at the SUNY College of Technology in Alfred, New York. He has received grants from the SUNY Research Foundation to develop teaching materials on the Sherlockian methods of problem solving and has delivered conference presentations on Sherlock Holmes at Colby College, the Stevens Institute of Technology, and Alfred University.

Richard is the author of three books about Sherlock Holmes and is a frequent contributor to THE BAKER STREET JOURNAL and THE SERPENTINE MUSE. His most recent book on the Great Detective is a collection of insightful essays titled VIGNETTES OF SHERLOCK HOLMES (Gryphon Books, 2008).

Dr. Kellogg delights in introducing young readers to the magical world of Sherlock Holmes and Dr. John Watson. He hopes that the exploits of Barry Baskerville will encourage children to explore the original tales of detection penned by Sir Arthur Conan Doyle. They will discover that Sherlock Holmes can be a marvelous companion for the rest of their lives.

AMERICAN SPORTS

When I was growing up in a small New Hampshire town in the 50s and 60s, we had a local radio personality named Jock McKenzie who was a bit of a celebrity. His three times a day radio report of local middle and high school sporting events was listened to by hundreds in a three city area. What I remember the most about his show was his parting line, "Next to religion, nothing contributes more to the American way of life than sports." That I should recall those exact words after all this time is more of a significance to their worth than my memory skills.

You see, I wasn't much of a sports enthusiast growing up and never belonged to any organized sport team. Most of my familiarity with such physical activities came from neighborhood pick-up games on summer afternoon and Fall evenings. Right next to our house was a huge baseball field used by several men's leagues in town and their games were usually early evening when daylight seemed to stretch until way past 8 p.m.

So, after lunch, my brother and I would gather a bunch of neighborhood kids, grab our bats, gloves and balls and head out to the pitcher's mound to divide up teams. Then we set about being Mickey Mantle or Willie Mays for three to four hours. Thinking about those afternoons brings a truly warm glow to my soul.

Still, the writer in me always recognized the drama inherent with any competitive contest. All one need do is study the lives of famous athletes from any sport, regardless of the ratings being amateur or professional, and soon you'll be uncovering true-to-life tales of heroism and sacrifice beyond imagination. Sports bring out in people their truest self—they are a field upon which lies and deceits have no part and only one's real talent, endurance and sacrifice will win out in the end. So ingrained is this in the American psyche, it is also a fact that in even defeat, one can become victorious. That's the real quality of sports all of us admire so much.

One of the things we here at Airship 27 Productions learned early in our studies of classic American pulps was the fact that American sports were a favorite subject of dozens of highly popular titles—be it the entire spectrum of professional activities or series that focused solely on one particular sport. Regardless, all were extremely popular among the readers of those bygone days. And it so it was inevitable that in fulfilling our own personal mission of bringing back all types of pulps we should eventually turn our attention to the world of sports. And here we are.

Four of our best writers have delivered a quartet of amazing 1930s sport stories which we know you are going to enjoy. Terrence McCauley, J. Walt Layne, John Rose and Fred Adams Jr. masterfully capture not only the time but carefully envision how some of these sports were played back when. Not an easy task by any means. Whereas no sooner had we assembled the fiction pieces than writer Richard Kellogg offered us a personal memoir he'd penned about his own youthful experiences learning to hunt deer with a favorite uncle. It was perfect tale to wrap up this premier issue of ALL-AMERICAN SPORTS STORIES.

Oddly enough, the art provided for this premier volume was provided to extremely talented artist of foreign origins. Canadian Art Cooper did the stunning black and white interior illustrations and New Zealand's own Shane Evans the magnificent collage cover painting. Finally Art Director Rob Davis gave the entire package a classic pulp mag look and we couldn't be happier with it.

So there you have it. Please, if you enjoyed this issue and would like to see more, then by all means drop us a line. We always love hearing from our loyal readers. Until then, let me wrap this up with a familiar cry: PLAY BALL!!!

Ron Fortier
Managing Editor
Airship 27 Productions
2/15/2016